"How about you don't leave?"

She'd been looking around the room, but now snapped her attention back to him. "What?"

"You heard me. Don't leave. Stay in my room. With me." He pulled her closer, resting his cheek on hers as he spoke into the delicate shell of her ear. "Spend the night in my bed, Penelope. You won't regret it."

Her hand tightened in his. "I—I can't. It's... inappropriate."

He pulled his face away from hers to find she looked as flustered as she sounded. Her eyes bounced from his face to his chest. Her steps faltered.

Zach dropped the pretense of dancing, and cradled her gorgeous face in both hands. "It's not only appropriate. It's expected. To this room of people, you're my future wife. I would never let my fiancée drive home alone this late."

A small smile found her face. "My God. You really are a caveman."

"Aw, honey," he said with a wink as he laced his fingers with hers. "But I'm your caveman."

* * *

Lone Star Lovers is part of the
Dallas Billionaires Club trilogy
from Jessica Lemmon!

Dear Reader,

It's with great pleasure that I introduce you to the Ferguson family: three stubborn siblings, each with their own stake in Ferguson Oil, and each brimming with personality. None of these billionaires planned on settling down, but one by one in the Dallas Billionaires Club series, oh, baby...they're going *down*.

In *Lone Star Lovers*, you meet the middle sibling, Zachary Ferguson, and his one-night stand turned fake fiancée turned baby mama. Penelope Brand is a public-relations maven whose job is to solve everyone else's problems, but she's having a difficult time getting herself out of this pickle in particular. Maybe because of the undying attraction she has to Zach, who has vowed to keep her near by any means possible...

As the CEO of Ferguson Oil, Zach knows how to get what he wants—and what he wants is Penelope. What he *doesn't* want is to risk his heart again, but he truly believes love and marriage don't have to coexist. Can't he marry her without sacrificing his heart?

I hope you enjoy the first book set in the Fergusons' world. If you do, I invite you to tell the world (or at least me) what you thought. You can find more information about my books on my often-updated website, www.jessicalemmon.com. You can also find me on Facebook at authorjessicalemmon, on Twitter, @lemmony, on Instagram at jlemmony and on Pinterest at lemmony.

Thanks a *billion* for reading,

Jessica Lemmon

JESSICA LEMMON

LONE STAR LOVERS

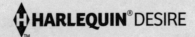

Recycling programs
for this product may
not exist in your area.

ISBN-13: 978-1-335-97138-8

Lone Star Lovers

Copyright © 2018 by Jessica Lemmon

Printed in U.S.A.

™ www.Harlequin.com

A former job-hopper, **Jessica Lemmon** resides in Ohio with her husband and rescue dog. She holds a degree in graphic design currently gathering dust in an impressive frame. When she's not writing supersexy heroes, she can be found cooking, drawing, drinking coffee (okay, wine) and eating potato chips. She firmly believes God gifts us with talents for a purpose, and with His help, you can create the life you want.

Jessica is a social media junkie who loves to hear from readers. You can learn more at jessicalemmon.com.

Books by Jessica Lemmon

Harlequin Desire

Dallas Billionaires Club
Lone Star Lovers

For Grandma Edie.
Thank you for putting that first Harlequin book
in my hands. I wish you were here
so I could put this one in yours.

One

Texas in the springtime was a sight to behold. The Dallas sunshine warmed the patio of Hip Stir, where Penelope Brand sat across from her most recent client. Blue cloudless skies stretched over the glass-and-steel city buildings, practically begging the city-dwellers to take a deep breath. Given that nearly every table was full, it appeared that most of downtown had obeyed.

Pen adjusted her sunglasses before carefully lifting her filled-to-the-brim café au lait. The mug's contents wobbled but she made that first sip to her lips rather than to her lap. Which was a relief since Pen always wore white. Today she'd chosen her favorite white jacket with black silk piping over a vibrant pink cami. Her pants were white to match, slim-fitting and ended in a pair of black five-inch stilettos.

White was her power color. Pen's clients came to her for crisis control—sometimes for a completely fresh start. As their public relations maven, a crisp, clean do-over had become Pen's specialty.

She'd started her business in the Midwest. Until last year, the Chicago elite had trusted her with their bank accounts, their marriages and their hard-won reputations. When her own reputation took a header, Pen was forced to regroup. That unfortunate circumstance was rapidly gaining ground as her "past." The woman sitting across from her now had laid the foundation for Penelope's future.

"I can't thank you enough." Stefanie Ferguson shook her head, tossing her dark blond ponytail to the side. "Though I suppose I should thank my stupid brother for the introduction." She lifted her espresso and rolled her eyes.

Pen smothered a smile. Stefanie's *stupid brother* was none other than the well-loved mayor of Dallas, and he'd called on Penelope's services to help his younger sister out of a mess that could mar his reputation.

Stef didn't share her brother's reverent love for politics and being careful in the public eye. She flew by the seat of her skinny jeans, the most recent flight landing her in the arms of one of the mayor's most critical opponents, Blake Eastwood.

Blake's development company wanted to break ground for a new civic center that Mayor Ferguson opposed. Critics argued that the mayor was biased, given the civic center was to be built near his family's oil wells, but the mayor's supporters argued the unneeded new-build would be a waste of city funds.

Either way, the photograph of Stefanie exiting a hotel, her arm wrapped around Blake's while they both wore wrinkled clothing and sexually satisfied smiles, had caused some unwanted media attention.

The mayor had hired Brand Consulting to smooth out the wrinkles of what could have turned into a PR nightmare. Penelope had done her job and done it well. One week after the snafu, and the media had already moved on to gossiping about someone else.

All in a day's work.

"You're coming to the party tonight, right?" Stef asked. "I'm looking forward to you being there so I have a girl to talk to."

Stef was younger than Pen by four years, but Pen could easily become close friends with her. Stef was smart, savvy and, while she was a tad too honest for her brother's taste, Pen welcomed that sort of frankness. Too bad a friendship with Stefanie broke Pen's most recently adopted rule: never become personally involved with a client.

That included an intimate friendship with the blonde across from her.

A pang of regret faded and faded fast as Pen remembered why she'd had to ink the rule in the first place. Her ex in Chicago had tanked her reputation, cashed her checks and forced her to journey to her own fresh start.

"I wouldn't miss it," Pen answered with a smile. Because yes, she wasn't going to become besties with

Stefanie Ferguson, but neither would she turn down a coveted invitation to the mayor's birthday party.

Those who gained entry to the mayor's annual soiree, held at his private gated mansion, were the envy of the city. Pen had worked with billionaires, local celebrities and sports stars in her professional past, but she'd never worked directly with a civil servant. Attending the most sought-after party of the year was as good as a gold star on her résumé.

Pen picked up the tab for her client and said her goodbyes to Stefanie before walking two blocks back to her office.

Thank God for the mayor's troublemaking sister.

Stepping in at the pleasure of Mayor Chase Ferguson might have been the best decision Pen had made since moving to Dallas. Her heart thudded heavily against her breastbone as she thought about what this could mean for her growing PR firm—and for her future as an entrepreneur. There were going to be many, *many* people at this party who would eventually require her services. The world of politics teemed with scandal.

After finishing her work for the day, she locked the glass door on her tenth-floor suite and drew the blinds. In her private bathroom, Pen spritzed on a dash of floral perfume and brushed her teeth, swapping out her suit for the white dress she'd chosen to wear to the mayor's party. She'd brought it with her to work since her apartment was on the other side of town and the mayor's mansion was closer to her office.

She smoothed her palms down the skirt and checked the back view in the full-length mirror on the door. *Not bad at all.* After way too much vacillating this morning, she'd opted for hair down versus hair up. Soft waves fell around her shoulders and the color of her pale blue eyes popped beneath a veil of black-mascaraed lashes and smoky, silver-blue shadow.

The dress was doing her several favors, hugging her hips and her derriere in a way that wasn't inappropriate, but showcased her daily efforts at the gym.

I couldn't let you leave without pointing out how well you wear that dress.

Shivers tracked down her arms and she rubbed away the gooseflesh as the silken voice from two weeks ago wound around her brain.

Pen had moved to Dallas thinking she'd sworn off men forever, but after nearly a year of working nonstop to rebuild her business, she'd admitted she was lonely. She'd been at a swanky jazz club enjoying her martini when yet another man had approached to try his luck.

This one had been a tall, muscled, delicious male specimen with a confident walk and a paralyzing green stare that held her fastened in place. He'd introduced himself as "Just Zach," and then asked to sit. She'd surprised herself by saying yes.

Over a drink, she learned they'd crossed paths once before—at a party in Chicago. They knew the same billionaire family who owned Crane Hotels, though she'd never imagined running into Zach again anywhere other than Chicago.

She also never imagined she'd ask him to come home with her…but she did. When one drink led to another, Penelope let him lead her out of the club.

What a night it'd been.

His kisses had seared, branding her his for those stolen few hours. Hotter than his mouth were the acres of golden muscles, and she'd reveled in smoothing her palms over his bulging pecs and the bumps of his abs. Zach had a great ass, a better smile, and when he left in the morning, he'd even kissed her goodbye.

Stay in bed and recover, Penelope Brand.

A dimple had punctuated one of his cheeks, and her laugh had eased into a soft hum as she'd watched Zach's silhouetted masculine form dress in the sunlight pressing through her white bedroom curtains.

Sigh.

It had been the perfect night, curing her of her loneliness and adding a much-needed spring in her step. Pen had felt like she could take over the damn world. Amazing what a few earth-shattering orgasms could do for a girl's morale.

She was still smiling at that memory of "Just Zach" from Chicago when she climbed behind the wheel of her Audi and started toward her destination. One night with Zach had been fun, but Pen wasn't foolish enough to believe it could have been more. As the daughter of entrepreneurs, success had been ingrained in Pen's mind from an early age. She'd taken her eye off the prize in Chicago and look what'd happened.

Never again.

At the gates of the mayor's mansion, Pen presented the shiny black invitation, personalized with her name in an elegant silver script, and smiled down at the slender silver bangle on her left wrist. It had been included with her invitation. Dangling from the bracelet was a letter *F*, and she'd bet her new shoes that the diamond set in the charm was a real one. Every first-time attendee received a gift from the mayor.

The security guard waved her through and she smiled in triumph. She was *in*. The world of politics was ripe with men and women who might need to hire her firm in the future, and she would make sure every guest knew her name by the end of the evening.

Pen passed her car keys to the valet and walked the cobblestone path to the mayor's mansion. The grounds were elegant, lined with tall, slender shrubberies and short, boxed hedges. Fragrant, colorful flowers were in full bloom thanks to an early spring. Looming oaks that'd been there since the Ferguson family earned their first dollar in Dallas, ushered her in.

Inside, she checked her wrap and tucked her clutch under her arm. When her turn came, an attendant walked her to the mayor for a proper introduction.

Standing before the mayor, was it any wonder the man had earned the hearts of the majority of Dallas's female voters? Chase Ferguson was tall, his dark hair pushed this way and that as if it couldn't be tamed, but the angle of his clean-shaven jaw and the lines on his dark suit showed control where it counted.

"Ms. Brand." Hazel eyes lowered to a respectable survey of her person before Chase offered a hand. She shook it and he released her to signal to a nearby waiter. "Stefanie is around here somewhere," he said of his younger sister. He leaned in. "And thanks to you, on her best behavior."

The mayor straightened as a waiter approached with a tray of champagne.

"Drink?" Chase's Texas accent had all but vanished beneath a perfected veneer, but Pen could hear the slightest drawl when he lowered his voice. "You'll get to meet my brother tonight."

She was embarrassed she didn't know a thing about another Ferguson sibling. She'd only been in Texas for a year, and between juggling her new business, moving into her apartment and handling crises for the Dallas elite, she hadn't climbed the Ferguson family tree any higher than Chase and Stefanie.

"Perfect timing," Chase said, his eyes going over her shoulder to welcome a new arrival.

"Hey, hey, big brother."

Now *that* was a drawl.

The back of her neck prickled. She recognized the voice instantly. It sent warmth pooling in her belly and lower. It stood her nipples on end. The Texas accent over her shoulder was a tad thicker than Chase's, but not as lazy as it'd been two weeks ago. Not like it was when she'd invited him home and he'd leaned close, his lips brushing the shell of her ear.

Lead the way, gorgeous.

Squaring her shoulders, Pen prayed Zach had the shortest memory ever, and turned to make his acquaintance.

Correction: re-acquaintance.

She was floored by broad shoulders outlined by a sharp black tux, longish dark blond hair smoothed away from his handsome face and the greenest eyes she'd ever seen. Zach had been gorgeous the first time she'd laid eyes on him, but his current look suited the air of control and power swirling around him.

A primal, hidden part of her wanted to lean into his solid form and rest in his capable, strong arms again. As tempting as reaching out to him was, she wouldn't. She'd had her night with him. She was in the process of assembling a solid bedrock for her fragile, rebuilt business and she refused to let her world fall apart because of a sexy man with a dimple.

A dimple that was notably missing since he was gaping at her with shock. His poker face needed work.

"I'll be damned," Zach muttered. "I didn't expect to see you here."

"That makes two of us," Pen said, and then she polished off half her champagne in one long drink.

Two

Zach schooled his expression—albeit a bit late.

Penelope Brand wore a curve-hugging white dress like the night he'd seen her at the club. He'd been there with a friend who had long since left with a woman. Zach hadn't been looking to hook up until he spotted Pen's upswept blond hair and the elegant line from her neck to her bare shoulders.

Seeing her hair down tonight dropkicked him two weeks into the past. Her apartment. The moment he'd tugged on the clip holding her hair back and let those luscious locks down. The way he'd speared his fingers into those silken strands, before kicking her door closed and carrying her to her bedroom.

He'd sampled her mouth before depositing her onto her bed and sampling every other part of her.

And he did mean *every* part.

They hadn't discussed rules, but each had known the score—he wouldn't call and she wouldn't want him to—so they'd made the most of that night. She'd tasted like every debased teenage fantasy he'd ever had, and she'd delivered. He'd left that morning with a smile on his face that matched hers.

When he'd stepped into the shower at home that morning, he'd experienced a brief pinch of regret that he wouldn't see her again.

Though, hell, maybe he *would* see her again given lightning had already stricken them twice. He hadn't wanted to let her get away that night at the bar—not without testing the attraction between them.

He felt a similar pull now.

"If you'll excuse me." His brother Chase moved off, arm extended to shake the palm of a round-bellied man who ruled half of Texas. As one-third owner of Ferguson Oil, it was Zach's job to know the powerful players in his brother's life—in the entire state—but this man was unfamiliar.

"Just Zach," Pen snapped, drawing his attention. Her blue eyes ignited. "I thought you were a contractor in Chicago."

"I used to be."

"And now you're the mayor's brother?"

"I've always been the mayor's brother," he told her with a sideways smile.

He'd also always been an oil tycoon. A brief stint of going out on his own in Chicago hadn't changed his parentage or his inheritance. When Zach had received a call from his mother letting him know his father, Rand Ferguson, had suffered a heart attack, Zach had left Chicago and never looked back.

He wasn't the black sheep—had never resented working for the family business. He'd simply wanted to do his own thing for a while. He had, and now he was back, and yeah, he was pretty damn good at being the head honcho of Ferguson Oil. It also let his mother breathe a sigh of relief to have Zach in charge.

Penelope's face pinched. "Are you adopted or something?"

He chuckled. Not the first time he'd heard that. "Actually, Chase and I are twins."

"Really?" Her nose scrunched. It was cute.

"No."

She pursed her lips and damn if he didn't want to experience their sweetness all over again. He hadn't dated much over the past year, but the way Penelope smiled at him had towed him in. He hadn't recognized her at first—the briefest of meetings at a Crane Hotel function three years ago hadn't cemented her in his mind—but there was a pull there he couldn't deny.

Pen finished her champagne and rested the flute on a passing waiter's tray. With straight shoulders and the lift of one fair eyebrow, she faced Zach again. "You didn't divulge your family status when I met you on Saturday."

"You didn't divulge yours."

Her eyes coasted over his tuxedo, obviously trying to square the man before her with the slacks and button-down he'd worn to the club.

"It's still me." He gave her a grin, one that popped

his dimple. He pointed at it while she frowned. "You liked this a few weeks ago." He gestured to himself generally as he leaned in to murmur, "You liked a lot of this a few weeks ago."

Miffed wasn't a good enough word for the expression that crossed her pretty face. The attraction was still there, the lure that had existed as they came together that night in her bed twice—no, wait, *three times*.

Zach decided he'd end tonight with her in his bed. They'd been good together, and while he wasn't one to make a habit of two-night stands, he'd make an exception for Penelope Brand.

Because *damn*.

"I'll escort you to the dining room. You can sit with me." He offered his arm.

Pen sighed, the action lifting her breasts and softening her features. Zach's grin widened.

So close.

She qualified with, "Fine. But only because there are a lot of people here I would like to meet. This is a business function for me, so I'd appreciate—"

The words died on Penelope's lips when a female shriek rose on the air. "Where is he? Where is that son of a bitch who owes me money?"

The crowd gasped and Pen's hand tightened on his forearm.

Zach turned in the direction of the outburst to find a rail-thin redhead in a long black dress waving a rolled-slash-wadded stack of paper in her hand. Her brown eyes snapped around the room, and her upper lip curled in a way that made him wonder how he'd ever found her attractive.

Granted she wasn't foaming at the mouth when they'd exchanged their vows.

"You." Her eyes landed on him as the security guards positioned around the house rushed toward her. Zach held up a hand to stop them. He'd try and talk Yvonne down from whatever crazy idea she'd birthed before they caused a bigger scene.

"V," he said, hoping to gain ground with the nickname he'd coined the night they met. A night soaked in tequila. "You're at my brother's birthday party. You have my attention. Is there something I can help you with?"

A big, bald security guy with an ugly scar down one cheek stepped closer to Yvonne, his mitts poised to drag her out the second Zach gave the signal.

"Write me a check for a million dollars and I'll be on my way." Yvonne cocked her head and waved the crumpled stack of papers in front of her. "Or else I'll tear up our annulment."

Tearing it up wouldn't make it go away. What was her angle?

"Marrying you entitled me to at least half your fortune, Zachary Ferguson."

It was laughable that she thought a million was *half*.

Penelope's hand slipped from his forearm and Zach reached over and put it back.

"Ex-wife," he corrected for Penelope's—hell, for everyone's—benefit. "And no, it doesn't."

"I'm going to make your life miserable, Zachary Ferguson. You just wait."

"Too late." He gave a subtle nod to the beefcake guard who circled Yvonne's upper arm in his firm grip as he warned her against fighting him.

To her credit, she didn't struggle. But neither did she go willingly. Yvonne's eyes sliced over to Penelope. "Who is this? Are you *cheating* on me?"

Here they went again. Yvonne had asked that question so many times in the two days they were married, Zach would swear she'd gone to bed sane and woken crazy.

He'd had the good sense to get out of the marriage, which was more than he could say for the sense he'd had going in. The details were fuzzy: Vegas, Elvis, the Chapel of Love, etcetera, etcetera... Getting married had seemed fun at the time, but spontaneity had its downfalls. Within twenty-four hours Yvonne had grown horns and a forked tongue.

"Make it two million dollars," Yvonne hissed, illustrating his point. The guard tugged her back a step, looking inconvenienced when she fought him.

Zach had money—plenty of it—but relinquishing it to the crazed redhead wasn't going to make her go away. If anything, she'd be back for more later.

"Get her out of here," Zach said smoothly, putting his hand over Pen's. "She's upsetting my fiancée."

"Your what?" Yvonne asked at the same time Penelope stiffened at his side.

"Penelope Brand, my fiancée. Yvonne, uh..." What was her maiden name? "Yvonne, my ex-wife." Yvonne's eyes burned with anger—flames Zach was only too happy to fan. "Penelope and I are engaged to be married. It's real, unlike what you and I had. You can contact my lawyers with any further questions."

Yvonne shrieked like the eels from *The Princess Bride* as security dragged her away.

Another security detail, this one slimmer but no less mean-looking, stepped in front of Zach.

"How the hell did she get in here?"

His eyes dipped to his shoes in chagrin before meeting Zach's angry expression again. "We'll call the police department, sir."

"No, don't. She's exuberant, but harmless." He took a breath. Who wanted to deal with the paperwork?

"Very well." Security Guy Number Two followed in the path of the beefy guy.

Chase took his place, using his extra two inches of height to scowl down at Zach. "Let me get this straight," his brother said in that exaggerated calm way he had about him. "You're engaged…and married?"

"*Was* married."

"You didn't tell me you were married."

"Well, it only lasted forty-four hours."

"And you—" Chase's hawk-like gaze snapped away from Zach to lock on Penelope "—didn't tell me you were engaged to my brother."

"I—" Pen started.

"It's not true." Zach couldn't bullshit a bullshitter, and his brother was in politics, so he was overqualified. "I wanted to refocus Yvonne's attention."

He would come clean with Chase, even though he'd

been left out of the loop where Stefanie was concerned. Zach had known Stef was having some issues but he didn't realize his brother had called in the cavalry in the form of Penelope's PR services.

"You succeeded," Chase said. He smiled amiably at Penelope. "Looks like you've secured your next client, Ms. Brand. I trust you can clean up my brother's mess."

A few truncated sounds that might have been Pen struggling for breath came from her throat, but she reined in her simmering argument to say, "Yes. Of course."

"Excellent." Chase lifted his voice to address the guests milling around the bar. "If everyone would find your seats in the dining room, dinner will be served shortly." He turned his attention back to Zach and Penelope. "I assume you two would prefer to sit together."

Zach simply smiled as he looked down at a wide-eyed Penelope. This evening had fun written all over it. "I wouldn't allow my fiancée to sit with anyone else."

Three

Penelope strolled into the oversize ballroom on Zach's arm. The mansion boasted enough round tables and slipcovered chairs to seat the mayor's one-hundred-plus guests. Similar to a wedding, there was a head table for the guests of honor. In this case those guests were Mayor Chase Ferguson, Stefanie Ferguson, Zach and the recent addition of Penelope.

The rectangular table was set apart from the others and dotted with votive candles and low vases with flower arrangements.

A few staff members from the mayor's office were also seated at the head table. A plucky, talkative woman named Barb, Roger, who looked and acted the part of secret service, and a scowling, large-framed man named Emmett Keaton.

Emmett, who had been introduced as the mayor's "friend and confidant," had short, cropped hair, a healthy dash of stubble on his face and eyed Stefanie with disdain the entire time he ate his pear and Gorgonzola salad. Stefanie had glared at him from her spot across the table before rolling her eyes and drinking down her white wine.

Clearly there was no love lost between those two.

Penelope wasn't surprised. Stefanie's recent scrape had drawn attention to the Ferguson family—and not the good kind. It would make sense that she wasn't favored among the mayor's staff.

Speaking of scrapes, Pen now had another to deal with in the form of Zach's ex-wife. Pen didn't know what shocked her more—that Zach had married the unhinged woman, or that he'd been married at all. It might be a tie.

Zach wasn't the marrying type. He was the one-night-stand type. Or so Pen had thought.

Slicing into the sun-dried-tomato-crusted rack of lamb on her plate, she kept her voice low and asked Zach the million-dollar question.

"Were you married when we slept together two weeks ago?"

His jaw paused midchew before he continued, smiling with his mouth shut, and then swallowed down the bite. He swept his tongue over his teeth and took a drink of water before responding. Pen didn't mind the delay. The lamb was spectacular. She sliced off another petite bite, this time plunging it into the ramekin of balsamic dipping sauce first.

"No," he finally said.

She patted her lips with her napkin. "When did it happen?"

"Last New Year's Eve." He glanced around the table, but no one was paying them any attention. Barb was chattering to Stefanie, and Emmett and Chase were having a low conversation of their own. Roger wasn't at the table any longer. When had he left? He was sneaky, but then—secret service, so it made sense.

"In Vegas," Zach finished.

Pen laughed, drawing Emmett's and Chase's attention before they returned to their conversation. "Cliché, Zach."

"Yeah, as was the annulment."

"And the need for our betrothal?"

Zach shrugged muscular, tux-covered shoulders. "You helped Stef. You're a good ally to have."

"You could have introduced me as an adviser. As anyone."

He stabbed a bite of meat with his fork and waved it as he said, "Fiancée had a nice ring to it."

"Very funny." Fiancée. Ring. At least his personality was the same as the night she'd invited him home with her. He'd been cheeky then, too.

She smiled, glued her eyes to his and enjoyed the sizzling heat in the scant space between them for the next three heartbeats. Then she focused on her food again.

Once the dinner dishes were cleared, dessert appeared in the form of a dark chocolate tart, a single, perfect raspberry interrupting a decadent white-chocolate drizzle.

"Speech time," Zach prompted his brother.

"Go get 'em, Tiger," Stefanie said, clearly teasing him.

Chase stood and buttoned his suit jacket, then glided to the podium. From her side of the table, Pen wouldn't have to so much as turn her head to watch. Unlike everyone else who had swiveled in their chairs.

Chase had great presence. Elegant. Regal. He talked and the world quieted to listen. She remembered the first time she'd seen him on television and thought—

A gasp stole her throat when warm fingers landed on her knee.

Zach.

Barb looked over her shoulder and offered a wide smile. Pen gave the other woman a tight nod as she reached beneath the table and removed Zach's wandering hand.

Pen cleared her throat and refocused on Chase's speech when Zach's fingers returned. This time she managed to stifle the surprised bleat in her throat. She slanted a glare to her right where he lounged, elbow resting on the arm of his chair, his fingers pressed to his lips and his eyes narrowed as if hanging on to every word his brother said.

With the fingers of Zach's other hand swirling circles on the inside of her knee, Pen couldn't concentrate on a single word of the speech. A quick glance around confirmed that no one could see what was happening beneath the tablecloth.

She shifted in her seat, but before she could crush his fingers between her kneecaps, he gripped her leg with a tight hold. She swallowed down a ball of thick lust as he pushed her legs apart.

Pen flattened her hands on the tablecloth as Zach's hand traveled from her knee and climbed the inside of her thigh. She closed her eyes, visions of the night they'd spent together flashing on the screen of her mind.

His firm, insistent kisses on her jaw, her neck and lower.

The deep timbre of his laugh when she'd struggled with his belt.

He'd ended up stripping for her while she sat on her bed and watched every tantalizing second.

She was snapped to the present when Zach's fingertips dug into the soft skin of her thigh, and without warning, brushed her silk panties. Pen fisted one hand on the tablecloth, dragging her dessert plate to the edge of the table. Her glass of red gave a dangerous wobble.

She held her breath when he touched her intimately again, the scrap of silk going damp against his pressing fingers. When he pulled her panties aside and brushed bare skin, Pen bit down on her bottom lip to contain a whimper.

Then the mayor's voice crashed into her psyche.

"To Penelope and my brother, Zach. Many congratulations on your engagement."

She jerked ramrod straight to find every set of eyes in the room on her and glasses raised.

"Cheers," Chase said into the microphone.

Stiff as a cadaver, Pen managed a frozen smile. Conversely, Zach moved like a sunbathing cat, lazily tossing his napkin on the table before taking Pen's napkin from her lap and standing.

He offered his hand and a smirk, and Pen prayed that

the flush of her cheeks would be taken for embarrassment at the attention.

Placing her palm in his, she surreptitiously tugged her skirt down and stood with him to accept the room's applause.

Smooth as butter, Zach pushed her dessert plate from its perch at the edge of the table, handed Pen her wineglass and lifted his own.

Then, they drank to their engagement.

"I like this." Zach touched the *F* dangling from Pen's bracelet with his thumb. "Makes me feel possessive."

Her hand in his, Pen swayed to the music.

He liked her hand in his. He liked her laugh and the sweet scent of her perfume tickling his senses. He liked the way she smoothly handled Barb's question about a missing engagement ring.

Where is your diamond ring, darling?

Oh, we didn't want to upstage the mayor on his big day.

Pen was the right partner to choose for this particular snafu. She was a woman at the top of her game. Touching her under the table and listening as her breaths shortened and tightened was a bonus.

"What are you grinning about?" she asked him now.

"I think you know."

She hummed, not confirming or denying. Like he said, top of her game.

He turned her to the beat of the music, pressing his palm flat on her back and drawing her closer. She came rather than resist him, which he liked a whole hell of a lot.

"It's kind of your brother to give first-time guests such decadent gifts," she commented, redirecting his attention back to the bracelet. She waggled their joined hands so the pendant moved against her pale skin.

"You think *that's* what this is for?" Zach joked as he clucked his tongue. "You don't know the underground Chase Ferguson birthday secret."

Her eyes widened slightly and he didn't say more. Finally, she broke. "Are you going to tell me or not?"

"Depends." He leaned in, his whisper conspiratorial. "Are you into multiple sex partners?"

"Zach!" she quietly scolded. A second later her lips parted in a laugh that warmed the very center of his chest. She took her hand from his shoulder to playfully shove his chest. If he wasn't mistaken, she lingered a bit over his pectoral before resting her hand on his shoulder once again. "You're impossible."

He hovered just over her lips, testing her. "You're wearing the first letter of my last name, Pen. That means you're mine."

Blue eyes turned up to his and for a second he thought she might give him the gift of saying, *Show me to your room.* She hadn't been the least bit shy the night she'd invited him home with her.

Instead those blues rolled skyward and she hedged with, "Caveman."

But she'd given him an inch not arguing that she was his.

"What *really* happens next?" she asked. The crowd was thinning. Only a few couples danced, while others ringed the bar or sat with their coffees at the cleared tables.

"Things wind down. Cigars are smoked. Bourbon poured. Stef and I have rooms here so we usually stay the night."

"Well, make sure you tell me when it's the proper time to leave. I don't want to overstay my welcome on my maiden voyage to the mayor's birthday party."

"How about you don't leave?"

She'd been looking around the room, but now snapped her attention back to him. "What?"

"You heard me. Don't leave. Stay in my room. With me." He pulled her closer, resting his cheek on hers as he spoke into the delicate shell of her ear. "Spend the night in my bed, Penelope. You won't regret it."

Her hand tightened in his. "I—I can't. It's…inappropriate."

He pulled his face away from hers to find she looked as flustered as she sounded. Her eyes bounced from his face to his chest. Her steps faltered.

Zach dropped the pretense of dancing, and cradled her gorgeous face in both hands. "It's not only appropriate. It's expected. To this room of people, you're my future wife. I would never let my fiancée drive home alone this late."

A small smile found her face. "My God. You really are a caveman."

"Aw, honey," he said with a wink as he laced his fingers with hers. "But I'm your caveman."

Her silken laughter as he led them to the bar was a good sign she'd join him upstairs when the night wound to a close. Zach wasn't ready to draw the curtain on their evening yet, but he was anticipating getting her alone again. He'd give her the best night of her life.

Well, assuming the last night they'd spent together could be topped.

It was a challenge he embraced.

Four

"We're turning in. Happy birthday." Zach offered his brother a hand and Chase shook it, which Penelope found charming though formal. She wondered if those two had ever wrestled or punched each other in the face when growing up, and then figured they probably had. It wasn't hard to imagine rough and tumble boys beneath their polished exteriors.

"Penelope, make yourself at home," Chase told her. "My staff will get you whatever you need."

"*I'll* get her what she needs," Zach said, taking her hand in his. "She's my fiancée."

At his offered wink, Pen let herself smile. Zach was a lot of things—more than she knew before she learned he was Chase Ferguson's brother—but among his top qualities, Zach was *fun*. Now that Pen had taken him on, she was breaking her cardinal rule of not sleeping with a client. She'd break it this time—if only for him. He made rule-breaking downright delicious. He focused her attention on the present. Which was the exact reason she'd invited him home that night at the club.

An inkling of warning that her ex had cost her everything vibrated at the back of her skull, but the champagne bubbles swimming in her tummy drowned it out.

Her situation with Zach was totally different. The fake fiancée act was a ruse, true, but she couldn't see a reason not to take advantage of another night with him. He'd been working that angle since he touched her under the table tonight.

Hand in hand they passed by Stefanie, who pushed her lip into an exaggerated pout. "I can't believe you didn't tell me you were engaged to this idiot." Stef shot a thumb toward Zach.

"Your secret-keeping skills are dubious," he grumbled.

They'd opted not to share the truth with Stefanie—Chase's idea. He thought it was better if she was in the dark like everyone else.

"You have a lot of secrets lately." Stef eyed Zach, her mouth pulling at the corners.

"So do you," he said. "I had no idea you were working with my beautiful fiancée on a cover-up."

"It wasn't a cover-up," Pen interjected before these two sniped away her good mood. "We simply rerouted the public's attention."

"Thank you for that." Stefanie gripped Pen's arm and squeezed. "In all seriousness, I'm happy for you two."

"Thanks, sis," Zach said as a wave of guilt crashed over Penelope. She didn't mind contorting public opinion but lying to Zach's sister felt...wrong.

"I'm not staying here tonight," Stef told them. "I have a date with another of my brother's mortal enemies."

Zach's shoulders went rigid, a wave of heat emanating from his form.

"Just kidding!" Stef's grin was wide. She bid them good-night and Pen stroked her hand up Zach's tuxedo jacket to soothe him.

"Down, boy."

His eyes snapped over to her, the heat there transforming from anger to lust—which was even more sinister.

"Boy?" Zach startled Pen by bending at the knees to lift her into his arms. The few guests left milling about reacted with gasps or soft laughs. Pen, eyes wide, held on to him, her fingers entwining in the thick blond hair at the back of his neck.

"Sounds like you need a reminder from the *man* who shared your bed a few weeks back."

His confident smile, strong arms and twinkling green eyes consumed her. She bit down on her lip and remembered all too well the details of that night. Nevertheless, she said, "I could, now that you mention it."

A smile spread his full lips.

Fake fiancée or not, for her, the attraction part of their relationship was very real. Penelope was going to take advantage of every exciting, promising part of it.

She barely had a moment to take in her surroundings when Zach's muscular chest was flush with her back.

He swept her hair off her neck and put his lips over her pounding pulse.

"I don't have an overnight bag," she breathed, tilting her head to give him better access.

His tongue covered her earlobe before he tugged with his teeth. Goose bumps rose on her skin and she reached up to palm the back of his head.

His mouth was as intoxicating as any liquor, but a thousand times more potent.

"I'll at least need—" a gasp stole her words as his hand coasted from her waist to the sides of her breasts, teasing her "—a toothbrush," she finished.

He replied to her complaint by sliding warm fingers over her bare back, then snicking the zipper of her dress down over her backside.

"Gorgeous. Damn, Pen. I love your ass."

"Likewise." She managed a breathy laugh and turned in his arms. The way he looked at her made her feel gorgeous. Like she was the only one he wanted in this world.

His fingers pushed into her hair and he cupped the back of her neck, pegging her with a serious green stare. "Tell me the truth."

"About?" She raised her eyebrows in curiosity.

"Have you thought of me in the past few weeks?"

"Yes."

Zach's palm warmed her neck and shifted upward until he cradled the back of her skull. He dipped his head but didn't kiss her, continuing his interrogation.

"Tell me what you thought about, Penelope Brand."

His dimple dented one cheek when he offered a lop-sided smile. "In graphic detail."

It was a smile she couldn't help returning. Her hands fisting the material of his shirt, she yanked it from his pants and stroked her hands along his hot, golden skin.

"You first," she whispered a hairsbreadth away from his lips.

She'd meant to be cute, but Zach's smile vanished. His other hand went to her back and, pressing her until her breasts flattened against his chest, he answered her.

"Every morning since I walked out of your apartment, I wake up hard and ready. The woman in my head missing her clothes has blond hair, pale blue eyes and your name."

His pupils dilated, the black darkening his surrounding green irises. "Your turn."

She remembered lots of things. The way he moved over her, the way he filled her, consumed her, during their lovemaking. But mostly the way he laughed and made her life fun for that slice of time.

He made her forget her obligations or the fact that she'd once let a man trample over her business and her good sense. Zach made her feel beautiful and cherished and hot. Really freaking hot.

"I remember," she started, tugging at his black leather belt, "your face when you came." She unfastened his pants and slipped her hand inside, gliding her palm along the thick ridge of his erection.

Zach's nostrils flared, his hands rerouting to her hips and digging in for purchase.

"You looked a lot like you do right now." She massaged

his manhood, tipping her chin to swipe her tongue along his bottom lip. That lip tasted like she remembered—warm and firm and laced with desire. "In control but in danger of losing it."

She'd meant to spur him on. He didn't disappoint.

He reached for the skirt of her dress and peeled it past her hips and stomach and over her head. He tossed it inside out to the floor.

"I'm in no danger of losing control, Ms. Brand," Zach informed her, his lazy Texas drawl intensifying. "But you are."

Her white lace bra was the next article of clothing to get the heave-ho. He disarmed the strap so quickly that in a blink both her breasts were bare, her nipples standing up, begging for his attention.

Attention they got.

Zach's arms looped her back and Pen had to move both hands to his shoulders when he dropped his mouth to sample a breast. His tongue swirled and suckled and she let her head fall back, losing herself in the moment. That was what he did to her—made her live in the right now and not beyond.

Who could resist?

He backed her across the room and she went, turning to take in the bed they were about to make very good use of. The regal four-poster frame reached for the ceiling above a pile of gold-and-maroon bedding and pillows fit for royalty.

Thighs against hers, Zach walked her two steps until her butt collided with the mattress. She sat, eyes tipped to his. He stood looking down at her, shirt untucked, pants open, eyes aflame.

"Damn, I don't know what to do first."

"I do." Pen reached for his cock again but Zach snatched her hand.

"Not that." His smirk was confident when he hooked his fingers into her panties and swept them off her legs. At her ankles, he paused, watching her as he tossed one of her tall shoes over his shoulder, then the other. The scrap of silk went next. With a tip of his chin, he said, "Scoot."

She did, naked and so excited she wondered if he could see the shake in her arms as she settled herself on the middle of the bed.

He unbuttoned his tuxedo shirt, his eyes taking inventory of her like she was his next meal. Shirt discarded, he pushed his pants and briefs to his ankles, kicking off his shoes and socks in the process.

Penelope had to struggle not to drool.

Zach's lean, muscular chest was as mouthwatering as in her memory, the scant bit of chest hair whirling around two flat brown nipples. His erection jutted proudly between slim hips, which gave way to thick thighs. She realized she'd become lost staring at his body and quickly jerked her attention to his face.

Didn't help.

His body was to die for, but the real panty-melter was the dimple indenting one cheek when he smiled. His jaw was firm and strong, at odds with the playful twinkle in his eyes. Some might say his hair was in need of a trim, but Pen preferred the longish style. Especially when he braced himself over her and a thick lock fell rakishly over his forehead.

One knee depressed the mattress, then another. Her mouth dropped open when he lowered his head to her stomach and swiped her belly button with the tip of his tongue.

Flames licked her core. This was the treat she'd enjoyed most with him, and when he dragged his tongue an inch lower on her tummy, a high-pitched gasp betrayed her.

"That's what I like to hear." He hoisted a brow as he pulled her knees apart and settled between her thighs. "Be as loud as you want. No one stays in this part of the house, but if they do, I want them to know exactly why you agreed to marry me."

"Your money?" Pen teased to break the thick band of sexual tension strangling her.

"Oh, you'll pay for that." He didn't offer another teasing lick, but buried his face between her thighs and doled out the promised punishment.

She took every lash she was owed, her fists mangling the duvet, her head thrashing on the pillows that one by one met their final resting places on the floor.

He wrung an orgasm from her without trying, and two more when he stepped up his game.

Panting, delirious with pleasure, Pen lazily opened her eyelids when he began climbing her body. Zach's lips coasted over her ribs, breasts and to her neck where he bit her earlobe.

"Still on the pill?" His heated breath coated her ear.

"Yes." She gripped his biceps, anticipation wriggling within. She wanted him. Now. Hell, five minutes ago.

He positioned his hips over hers, his erection pressing into her pelvis and so very close to home.

"Have you been with anyone since our night together?"

The question pulled her out of the moment and she frowned ever so briefly.

"I haven't, Pen," he told her, sincerity on his face. "Unless you count my hand and a few showers where I tried to erase the memory of you."

He'd…thought about her. He was telling the truth.

Firm lips coasted over hers and a whisper of breath coated her mouth when he asked for her answer again.

"Have you?"

"No," she answered.

She was rewarded with the roll of Zach's hips and the feel of him sliding deep, overtaking her, filling her like she remembered.

His low groan reverberated against her breasts as she clung to his back, their bodies sealed by a thin layer of sweat.

He uttered a harsh curse that sounded a lot like a compliment before pushing his fingers into her hair and focusing his eyes on hers.

"You're mine, Pen."

Her eyes went to the bracelet sliding up her wrist when she looped her arms at his neck. The letter *F* dangling there like a brand.

"Say it," he demanded, claiming her with another deep thrust.

"I'm yours."

Another thrust had her pulse thrumming anew between her legs.

"Whose?" he growled, picking up the pace. All of her overheated. She knew what he was asking. Knew what he wanted. Pen threw her head back and gave him the answer he'd earned.

"Yours."

"Say my name, beautiful."

She did, on a shout. "Zach!"

The slide of his body against hers, the feel of his breath in her ear, the heat of his mouth on hers took her to new heights.

On another cry, she came again, and one more thrust brought forth his release. Sobering from her own tumble down Mount Orgasm, Pen watched Zach's face contort into pleats of pleasure. The way his eyes squeezed closed, his lips peeled back from his teeth while his powerful body shook.

The almost surprised expression and awestruck wonder in his eyes.

He watched her for the space of a few heartbeats and then a familiar smile crested his handsome face.

She returned it, equally awestruck. Equally pleased.

Five

The morning after the party, Zach woke in the guest bedroom next to Pen, in the bed they'd all but destroyed the previous night. The comforter and blankets were on the floor, the remaining sheets twisted and pulled from three corners, revealing the naked mattress.

He was also naked and sporting the morning wood he'd bragged to Penelope about, but this time instead of him taking the problem in hand, she was willing to alleviate it for him.

She slid down his body and he watched her pretty blond head bob over his thighs, eliciting so much pleasure, he thought he might never recover.

He did, though.

Enough to make love to her again and talk her into

a shared shower en suite. Soaping Pen's body could become his new favorite pastime.

Dressed in the white, albeit wrinkled, dress from last night, she looked like a woman who'd been claimed. Zach liked that look on her a hell of a lot. He liked learning she hadn't been with anyone since him more. Not only because he hadn't moved on from her yet, but also because that meant they could have sex without a condom, which was his other favorite pastime with her.

He took her hand and walked with her down the staircase. His brother was dressed in a suit, and it wouldn't surprise Zach to learn that he was working—even on a Saturday. Zach had pulled on a pair of pressed trousers and a button-down, but Chase had gone full-on jacket and tie.

His brother took in Zach and Pen as they entered the foyer, pausing with his cell phone in hand to smirk knowingly.

"Good morning, Zach. Penelope."

"Mayor," she said, chin held high.

Zach admired the hell out of her for that. In last night's clothes, her hair sexily rumpled and cheeks pink from their steamy shower this morning, Pen didn't care what Chase thought about her sleeping with his only brother.

"I have a meeting in thirty minutes," Chase informed Zach, his gaze returning to his phone. "Legislature for…"

He trailed off as he ran his thumb along the screen. His expression blanked, accentuating his pallor.

"Chase?" Zach asked, alarm rising within. "Is there a problem?"

Chase blinked and offered a tight smile. "An old friend." He gestured with the phone. "Haven't thought of her in a long time."

Her? Chase had a few *hers* in his past, but there was one more noteworthy than the others. But it couldn't be...

Zach wasn't going to find out anytime soon. Chase exited his house and climbed into the back seat of a town car idling out front.

"Sounds mysterious," Pen commented at Zach's side, curiosity outlining her pursed lips. Without digging deeper, she leaned in for a kiss and he gladly obliged. "I'm going to go. Thanks for...everything."

"Don't tell me you work today, too?"

She paused at the door and looked over her shoulder. "Your ex-wife situation isn't going to go away on its own."

Zach looped her arm in his. "I'll walk you out."

The valet had moved Pen's car next to his in the cobblestone drive. Her white Audi sat gleaming next to his black Porsche. He opened her car door but before he closed her inside, stole another kiss for the road.

"You'll be hearing from me, Mr. Ferguson."

"I'll be expecting a full report, Ms. Brand."

She looked sleepy and adorable, as well she should after he'd kept her up all night. He opened his mouth to add that he was in no hurry for her to wrap things up with Yvonne, but instead he backed away and watched as she drove off.

* * *

A week later Zach was sitting in his office, Penelope on the other side of his desk. She'd come to Ferguson Oil to discuss the details of the Yvonne Tsunami, which was swallowing up way too much of his time.

The arrangement was far from the way he wanted to spend time with Pen. For starters, she was way too clothed for his taste, and secondly, his brother was brooding in the corner, arms folded over his suit.

Zach stood in frustration the moment Pen stopped talking.

"I won't do it," he said, his words clipped.

"Hear her out," Chase advised from his position near the window. Dallas's cityscape shone outside in the sunny day, several buildings dwarfed from Zach's top-floor vantage.

"I heard her out," Zach told his meddling brother. He softened his voice with Pen, but kept a position of strength when he leaned over his desk to address her where she sat in his guest chair. "I'm not giving Yvonne any money."

"Zach…" Her pink mouth parted to argue and he cut her off.

"No." His desk phone chirped and he pushed a button. "Yes, Sam?"

His male assistant rattled off the name of an investor who was waiting on the line.

"Zach will call him back," Chase called loud enough to be heard.

"Yes, sir." Sam clicked off.

Zach sent his brother a death glare. Chase was unperturbed. He was in one of the highest ranks of government. A wilting glare from his younger brother wasn't going to rankle him anytime soon.

"Listen." Penelope stood, eye level with Zach since he was still looming over the desk. Her pale blue eyes locked with his and she softened her voice. "Yvonne has threatened to make more noise about your marriage. This could not only harm your newly minted position as Ferguson Oil's CEO, but also put a dent in the mayor's approval rating."

Zach fought a growl. Chase's mayoral reputation had been overshadowing everything for the past decade. God, how Zach hated politics. Unfortunately, he loved his brother, so he had a feeling this wouldn't be the last time he did something he didn't want to do for Chase's career.

"It's a relatively small amount of money to ensure her silence," Pen continued. "The world knows you were married, but I wouldn't put it past her to make up a few unbecoming stories and share them on social media. I've seen exes go public with false facts before." Her eyebrows lifted in determination.

"And if she goes against the agreement?" Chase asked, stepping into their tight circle.

"She'll have to pay Zach ten times the amount we're paying for her silence."

Chase and Zach exchanged glances.

"Short of that," Pen said, folding her arms to mirror Chase. "Zach could get ahold of a time machine and steer clear of the Chapel of Love last New Year's Eve."

"I don't like it," Zach told both of them.

"You don't have to like it. You just have to do it."
Pen's voice was tender, reminding him of the gentle way
she moaned when he was in bed with her three days
ago. When he'd struck the pretend fiancée agreement
with her, he'd hoped they'd share a bed more often than
once a week. She'd been doing a good job of avoiding
him on that front.

"Zach." Chase's voice crashed into Zach's fantasy
about the blonde in front of him.

"Fine," he said between his teeth. "Now get out."

Chase let the command roll off him. "I have a lunch
with important people. Penelope. Thank you."

"Anytime, Mr. Mayor." When he was gone, the door
shut behind him, Zach breached the few inches sepa-
rating him and Pen, tugged her by the nape of the neck
and kissed her mouth. She hummed, her eyelids droop-
ing in satisfaction.

"Where have you been hiding?" He thumbed her
bottom lip when she pulled back too soon.

"I've been working. On your problems and a few
others."

"None are my sister's I take it?"

"No." She shouldered her purse and tucked away
her cell phone. "None are Stefanie's. She's been on her
best behavior."

"Have dinner with me," he said as she pivoted on
one high, high heel.

Pen peeked over her shoulder and Zach allowed his
gaze to trickle down her fitted white jacket and short
white skirt. Her platinum-blond hair was in a ponytail

at the back of her head, the smooth length of it brushing her shoulder when she turned her head.

"I'm… I have to check my schedule."

"You have to make an appearance with me. Especially if we're going to approach Yvonne with a deal." Yvonne believed Zach and Pen were engaged. Everyone who'd attended his brother's party believed they were engaged.

"Okay. Dinner."

He pulled his shoulders back, proud to get a yes out of the evasive woman in front of him. His eyes dipped to the cleavage dividing the neckline of a sapphire blue shirt.

"And after dinner, you can come home with me."

She opened her mouth, maybe to protest, but smiled in spite of herself. He tucked two fingers into her shirt and pulled her closer, brushing her perky breasts.

"I'll make you breakfast in the morning," he told her. "And afterward, I'll make you something to eat."

She rolled her eyes but a soft chuckle escaped her. It was a yes if he'd ever heard one.

"I'll pick you up at your place at seven."

"I have to work late."

Zach was already back at his desk. "No. You don't. Seven o'clock."

He punched a button and summoned Sam. "Make reservations at One Eighty for myself and Ms. Brand for seven this evening."

"One Eighty?" Pen's brow rose. Was she impressed? He hoped so.

"Have you been?"

"Once. With a client who shall remain nameless."

"A male client?" he asked before he could stop himself.

Her Cheshire cat smile held. "Wouldn't you like to know?"

"Seven," he reiterated.

"Seven." She walked out of his office and Zach watched her go, looking forward to viewing her over candlelight the next time they saw each other. His phone beeped and Sam announced that the investor had called back.

Zach picked up the phone, but by the time he lifted his head, Pen was gone, his office door whispering shut.

Six

One Eighty was named for its half-circle shape. The restaurant hovered over Dallas, on the eighty-eighth floor of one of the city's most shimmering skyscrapers.

Outside the smudgeless windows, deep blue skies were losing their light and the moon was making its nightly appearance.

Pen had stopped working at five, unusual for her, but then so were billionaire dinner dates that were personal rather than solely business.

"How are your prawns?" Zach, fork and knife in hand, leaned over his steak dinner to ask.

"Delightful. How is your strip?"

"Fantastic."

They shared a grin over the low candlelight, and a

ping of awareness that started in Pen's stomach radiated out until it created a bubble around her and Zach.

Along with that ping of awareness came a lower, subtler thrum of warning.

She liked him. A lot.

Their chemistry was off the charts in bed, but also out of it.

She could've easily dismissed him as a playboy—a charmer who knew what to say to get a woman out of her clothes. Admittedly, Zach had done just that. But along with getting her out of her clothes, he'd also made a point to keep her in his life.

After what went down with her ex-boyfriend, Cliff, in Chicago—where she'd quite literally been bamboozled by a smooth-talking charmer—she should be wary of Zach.

But she wasn't wary.

Maybe it was because she'd gotten to know his brother, the mayor, and Stefanie, his sister. Maybe it was because of the way Zach had asked her to dinner when he full well could have invited her to his place.

She'd have said yes either way.

Did he know that?

She sliced into her shrimp dinner—buttery, garlicky, lemony heaven. "I contacted Yvonne today and let her know you were willing to talk about—"

"Penelope."

Fork hovering over her plate, she hazarded a glance at her date. Zach didn't look perturbed as much as patient.

"Sorry," she said. "I want to get this over with."

His eyes narrowed, eyelashes a shade darker than his hair obliterating his gorgeous green stare. "With Yvonne, yes. You and I? Not so much."

When she'd called him a caveman at the mayor's party, she hadn't been far off the mark. But she saw no reason to argue the point. The fact was she would wrap up the issue with Zach's ex-wife and then they'd have no reason to see each other. She'd make her services available for Chase or for their party-loving sister, but Pen and Zach had an expiration date.

So why are you here?

Excellent question.

"Did you pack a bag like I asked?" Zach lifted his wineglass, which was as foreign as the black shirt and black suit combo. She'd been so sure at that jazz club that she'd run into a blue-collar guy moonlighting in slacks. Now that she'd seen him in tuxes and suits, her brain scrambled to make sense of it.

He'd seemed safer when he was a contractor. Before she learned of his bank account or his heritage.

Nevertheless...

"I packed a change of clothes, yes." She took a dainty sip from her own wineglass. While she wasn't sure how to define what she and Zach had or to know how long they had access to it, she wasn't going to miss the opportunity to fill her head and heart full of sexy, vivid memories that would last if not a lifetime, at least a few years.

"Good. I want to show you my place. I think you'll like it." He took another bite of his steak, but not before dragging it through his mashed potatoes. A steak and potatoes guy. She shook her head as she tried to merge the two versions of Zach she thought she knew.

"Why did you leave Chicago? You seemed...at home there."

"I like the city. I liked the work more," he said. "But my family needed me, so I came home."

"Do you mean Stefanie?" She could imagine the youngest Ferguson sibling asking for his help.

"No. She leans on Chase." His smile took on a slightly sad quality. In a firmer voice, he added, "My father's heart attack required surgery and a long recovery. He was under strict orders not to return as acting CEO of Ferguson Oil."

"Doctors," Pen said with a roll of her eyes.

"Worse. My mother." Half of Zach's mouth pulled to one side in good humor, his dimple shadowing his stubbled cheek. She liked him a touch unkempt. "Once Dad was benched, that left me to work for the family business. Chase is obviously busy and Stef is obviously uninterested. She'll grow out of it."

Pen couldn't imagine Stef giving up her life as a socialite heiress to go into the oil business, but she kept that thought to herself.

"What about you?" Zach asked, turning the tables on her. She'd seen that possibility coming and had already decided she wouldn't deflect. She'd been eager to leave her life behind in Chicago, but face it—the internet was alive and well. If Zach typed her name into Google, he'd learn about her association with Cliff.

Still, she inhaled deeply before telling him the sordid, slightly embarrassing tale.

"Ever heard of the phrase 'the plumber's pipes are always leaking'?"

"The cobbler's children have no shoes?"

"Same idea." She laughed, already feeling better about

confessing. She sobered quickly. "I had a PR problem I couldn't spin."

Zach's eyebrows lowered. He didn't know.

"Cliff Goodman started out as a client. He hired me to repair his business's reputation when he was accused of dishonest practices." She'd believed him at the time—the research she'd done on him pointed to his upstanding reputation. "Once the issue was handled, he and I started dating and then—" she lifted her wine and ripped off the Band-Aid "—he became involved in my public relations business."

Her date's face darkened. Pen looked away from his intense stare. Diners quietly chatted at their tables, points of candlelight dotting the dimly lit room, mimicking the city lights outside the windows. The blue sky had gone black.

"Long story short, he went from involved to over-involved. I found out he'd been meeting with my clients in my place, cashing their checks and never following through. He left the city with a lot of my money after destroying my hard-won reputation. I didn't want to leave Chicago, but I didn't want to stay, either."

"Why Dallas?"

"A college friend of mine started an organic cosmetic company. She lives here and needed help maintaining her pure reputation in the face of a nasty divorce. So she hired me."

"And you stayed."

"I did."

They shared a silent moment. Pen wondered if he was thinking what she was thinking—that had it not been for her friend Miranda's phone call, Pen and Zach may never have seen each other again.

"It's a beautiful city." Pen swallowed some more wine, smoothly changing the subject.

"You're beautiful in it."

See? When he said things like that, she forgot all about her past and her rules and her personal struggles.

She forgot everything—including her promise to herself about not letting a client get too close. Especially a male client.

The waiter approached after they'd finished their plates.

"Madame, sir," the older man greeted, hands clasped in front of him. "Might I interest you in our fine dessert selections, or perhaps a glass of port wine or coffee?"

"No," Zach answered for them. "We'll pay and be on our way. My compliments to the chef."

"Such a gentleman," Pen teased.

"I grew up right." He leaned over the table and then, tossing the idea of his humble upbringing on its ear, took her hand and murmured, "I'm making you my dessert, tonight."

"Your post-dessert dessert." Zach's hand appeared from behind Pen, a glass of port wine in his grip. "It's a tawny, which I prefer. That bit of vanilla goes a long way."

She accepted the miniature wineglass and a kiss to her cheek. Zach rounded the enormous brown leather couch wearing nothing at all, another miniature glass dwarfed in his large hand.

Pen wasn't wearing anything, either, but had curled up in a blanket she'd found tossed over his ottoman. A blanket she now opened to include Zach. He accepted, cradling one of her breasts and delivering a tender kiss to the side of her mouth.

They'd stepped foot in his expansive apartment and stripped off each other's clothes in record time. She hadn't so much as seen the bedroom yet, though she did make a quick stop to the bathroom. Zach's apartment was a manly array of exposed brick, lights suspended from long, metal rods, his furniture deep browns and grays. The overall vibe was more industrial than rustic, yet had warmth that mirrored the owner himself.

She sipped the super-sweet wine, savoring the vanilla notes that Zach mentioned and quirking her lips at the way her dress had been haphazardly tossed over a chair along with Zach's discarded suit. Their shoes made a line from the foyer to the living room, the first articles of clothing they'd kicked off.

"You have a really nice apartment."

"Thanks."

"No billionaire mansion for you?"

"Nah, that's Chase's style."

"What about Stef? Does she tend toward high-rise apartment or sprawling mansion with horses and twenty-two bathrooms?"

"See, you think you're being cute, but my parents' house has twenty-two bathrooms."

"I know." She sipped her wine and peered over the tiny rim at Zach. "I looked them up and their house was in *Architectural Digest*. It's incredible."

"It's ridiculous. But my mother likes to redecorate. With thirty-seven thousand square feet, she's never at a loss for a room to have painted or altered to her ever-changing preferences."

Zach leaned back on the sofa, his arm draped around Pen. She snuggled closer and he adjusted the blanket to cover them both.

"Do you get along with them? Or are you the classically overlooked middle child?"

A low laugh that might have been confirmation bobbed his throat. "I get along with them. I joke about my mother's frivolity, but she's a great mother. My dad became sick and her world stopped on a dime."

"How is he now?"

"Good. Misses his bacon and sausage."

"And strip steaks?" she teased.

"It's Dallas, sweetheart. Men eat steak."

"Right. Heaven forbid you do something as effeminate as not eat a cow." She grinned, liking the way she could volley back at him. He was one of the easiest people she'd ever been around.

He moved in on her again and the kiss lasted a little longer than either of them intended. "Glad you packed a bag, Penelope Brand."

Her heart kicked into overdrive when Zach set aside his wine and took her wineglass from her hand. His insistent kisses peppered down her throat and collarbone. When he reached her stomach, his hand flattened on the space between her breasts and he pushed her to her back.

Then he lifted one of her legs onto his shoulder and made her dessert.

Again.

Seven

"Tell me everything," Miranda's bubbly voice, on speakerphone, filled Pen's office.

Pen had called her friend to thank her for the generous basket she was now digging through. She pulled out a tube of lipstick and spun it to examine the lush red color.

"I love this lipstick. 'Red Rum,'" she read off the bottom of the tube with a laugh. Sassy. That was Miranda.

"It's long-wearing, not tested on animals and one hundred percent organic. Now, if you don't tell me everything about the man you've been having sex with for the last month, I'm going to come to your office with torture implements."

She laughed at her friend's colorful description. Pen had casually mentioned Zach and that she'd been seeing him.

"It was supposed to be one night, and then we had a two-week gap." She lifted the basket from her desk and put it on the couch. She was *so* giving herself a makeover later. "But when I saw him again at the mayor's party, well… I couldn't help starting up with him again."

"And you ended up engaged! It's a fairy tale. It's a fantasy!"

It was a load of crap, but Pen had to keep up the facade with everyone.

"Yes, I was very surprised." That, at least, was the truth.

"I'll bet. Zachary Ferguson is one yummy prospect if you don't mind my saying. And he must be a real catch for you to have leaped in with both feet so soon."

"Yes," Pen said, unable to trot out any more false explanations.

"Listen, doll, I have to go. We're working on the spring line and I have an appointment."

"Thank you again for the gift."

"You bet. I expect a wedding invitation."

Pen opened her mouth to make an empty promise, but Miranda clicked off. With a sigh, she cleaned a few pieces of crinkled pink paper that had been used as packing in her gift basket from her planner pages.

May's schedule wasn't as full as she'd like it to be, but she had a few phone calls to return. She turned to her weekly page and checked off the line item that read "call Miranda," eyes skimming past the list of messages she'd written down to return on Monday but hadn't gotten the chance. And here it was Friday already.

Halfway to dialing a number for Maude Braxton,

Pen's eyes landed on a tiny red heart beneath Monday's date, and she frowned.

She'd been on birth control pills since she was a teenager because of erratic periods, and since she'd been on birth control pills, her cycle was correct down to the minute.

She hastily flipped back to April, located the red heart, and counted the days to today.

She was five days late.

Five. Days.

"Oh, my God." Her stomach tightened, her mind racing. Could she be…? No. No way. She was on the pill. And even if her trusted form of birth control failed her, she was in her early thirties. At her age it was normal for things to go haywire. There could be a perfectly good explanation. Stress. It could totally be stress. But when she flipped back to April and saw the name of a jazz club scheduled for eight p.m., another *perfectly good explanation* came to mind.

This one an even better explanation for a missed period.

Numbly, she stood from her desk and pulled her purse out from behind the basket overflowing with tubes of lipsticks, moisturizers and eye shadow palettes. So much for giving herself a makeover.

Pen was off to buy a pregnancy test.

Penelope's wine sat untouched in front of her, but she couldn't bring herself to say no and raise Zach's suspicions. Even though telling him he was going to be the father of their unborn child was the very reason she was sitting here with him. She'd successfully avoided him all weekend, which wasn't easy. It took a lot of circumventing on her part, but she had to wrap her head around the unfathomable truth.

Despite being on the pill the entire time she and Zach were together, that night after the jazz club, one of his swimmers had reached its goal.

"I have a charity dinner on Friday. Come with me." He sat on one corner of the wrap couch rather than in the middle next to her, and for once she was grateful for the space. "Chase and several of the Dallas brass who attended his party will be there. Good networking opportunity. Plus, now that we've wrapped up everything with Yvonne, it's best that we're seen together."

"Right." Pen somehow managed the one-word response despite her heart being lodged in her esophagus. He was right. It made sense to continue seeing him. If they mysteriously ended their engagement right when Yvonne had agreed to keep her trap shut, no one would believe it was real. Which might not matter except that Chase had announced to one and all that his brother was going to be married. She didn't want to be responsible for making Dallas's trustworthy mayor into a liar. If that wasn't enough public attention, there was the business world wagging their tongues about Ferguson Oil's youngest CEO taking a wife. Soon they'd have to amend their announcement to add that Zach had impregnated his bride-to-be…who the public would later learn wasn't going to be his wife at all.

God. This was a nightmare.

Maybe she didn't have to tell him today. Hope

sparked fresh in her chest. She had a good four weeks before her baby bump made itself known. Why not avoid him until then? And the paparazzi and public functions… She could become a hermit.

If she folded up the shingle on her PR business.

Sigh. That wasn't a realistic plan at all.

The only certainty was that she was keeping the baby. Her pregnancy was unexpected, yes, but Penelope believed deep in her soul that life unfolded in the order it did for a reason. If fate decided she was to be a mother, then she'd accept. It was as simple, and terrifying, as that.

Zach drank from his beer glass and eyed Pen's untouched wine. There was no way to avoid him for an extended period of time. He was a force—he was in her life. She had to do the mature thing and tell him the damn truth.

She filtered through her muddy mind until she located the speech she'd practiced in her office's bathroom mirror five times before she came here tonight. It was short, sweet and to the point.

"I'm pregnant."

Zach's limbs were stiff and unmoving, the blood sloshing against his eardrums making Pen's voice sound a mile away.

"I found out Friday night and I couldn't tell you over the weekend until I decided what to do. So here I am." Pen fastened her gaze on the wineglass. The wine she couldn't drink because she was *pregnant with his child.*

He focused on the beer glass in his hand for an ex-aggerated beat before managing, "What do you mean?"

His tone was as flat as the firm line of his pretend fiancée's unsmiling mouth. Pale blue eyes rested on his as if she was as shell-shocked as him. Only she couldn't be, because she'd been processing for three days and he'd had three seconds.

"I mean I'm having the baby—*your* baby. Keeping this a secret from you was never an option."

Hell, no, it's not, came the immediate thought.

He hadn't sat around and contemplated fatherhood, but now that he knew it was a reality, the surety of being involved rang tuning-fork true in the pit of his gut.

"The due date is December, right before Christmas." She shared it like she was talking about some other couple who was suddenly expecting a bundle of joy. For as distant as he felt from this announcement, she might as well be talking about someone else.

He set his beer aside and stood, unable to sit any longer. His measured steps were more of a stalk, but he reined in his energy to face the woman on his couch. Penelope had radically changed his future—his entire family's future—in a few short weeks.

Wait. Weeks? He did some quick math.

"It's been a little over two weeks since my brother's party. How the hell could you know you're pregnant already?"

Her porcelain skin went pink. "It's been *four* weeks, Zach, since you and I had sex the first time."

The first time?

Ah, hell.

He nodded to himself as reality reared its head. That was the clincher about math—the answer wasn't up for debate.

The jazz club. The night he'd explored her up and down and up again. The night he thought would be the last he saw of her.

He pulled a hand down his face, pausing with it over his mouth for a moment. His shock was a palpable entity swirling the room, his thoughts ranging from excitement to horror to wanting to accuse her of attempting to take his money like his ex-wife.

But this was Penelope he was talking about. Even if he didn't trust her—and he did—there was the significant matter of her not knowing he had that many zeroes in his bank account the night he took her back to her place.

"I have a plan," she said.

"A plan." Mind racing, his vision blurred as his thoughts circled the track again.

"I'm a public relations superhero, Zach. I have a plan." She patted the cushion next to her. He sat, but not next to her, and lifted his beer to take a hearty gulp. Hell, he might drink Pen's wine, too.

"It's simple. Over the next two weeks, you and I will be seen together less and less until we aren't seen together at all. We'll share a press release that you and I will not be raising the child together. We could even go with a story that we were friends and I wanted a child and you didn't and—"

"No." Zach's voice was thunderous, bouncing off the high ceilings and echoing around the room.

Pen's mouth was frozen midspeech for a second before she said, "I don't expect you to take on a baby.
You're a CEO with a budding career. What we had—"

"Have."

Her slim eyebrows rose. "Pardon?"

"What we *have*. Present tense."

"What we *have* is a month-long, on-and-off sexual
relationship."

"Until five minutes ago, that was true." She might
have alarmed him with unexpected news, but his brain
was now sliding into operation mode.

"I didn't mean for this to happen."

"That makes two of us."

"I came here to reassure you that I'm not coming
after your money." She stood suddenly. He stood with
her. She thrust her chin out, pride gleaming in her slitted eyes. "Plenty of working mothers manage to raise a
child alone. I certainly don't need your wealth to do it."

"This isn't a challenge," Zach said, his voice firm.
"I don't doubt you're capable of doing whatever you
damn well set your mind to, but know this." With his
thumb and forefinger, he tipped her chin up. "My child
growing in your belly isn't insignificant to me. I'm not
walking away."

From you or our baby.

None of the determination slipped from her gaze but
tenderness joined it. "I'd never deny you the right to
see or support your child, Zach. I was suggesting that
I get out of the way."

"Whose way are you in, Penelope?"

She didn't say it but he could feel the word *yours* in the tense air between them.

He dipped his face and captured her lips, sliding his tongue into her mouth and claiming her as his yet again. She wouldn't be eschewing herself from his presence anytime soon.

In fact...

He bent and scooped her into his arms never breaking their lip-lock as he made a path for the bedroom. He was going to see to it that she didn't get any farther away than his apartment.

Baby or no, he'd staked a claim on the blonde in his arms long before her surprise announcement.

And now she'd given him another reason to convince her to stay.

Eight

Penelope wasn't aware the charity dinner Zach invited her to would be at his parents' home. Until they pulled into the long driveway, fountains flanking either side, the grass mowed into an artistic crisscross pattern.

The house was gargantuan. She hadn't been joking about seeing it online, but one couldn't fathom thirty-seven thousand square feet until looking right at it. The place was like its own city.

"Wow," she murmured, gripping her wrap and clutch. "This is impressive."

From beside her in the back of the limo, Zach emitted a noncommittal grunt.

"Did you grow up in this house?"

"No. They bought this place about seven or eight years ago. We grew up in a big house, but not this big."

The driver pulled to a stop and an attendant in a fine tuxedo opened the limo door for her. She accepted his offered hand, stepped out and transferred that hand to Zach.

"You've done this before," he commented. His tux was like the one he'd worn to Chase's birthday party, but he'd chosen an all-black ensemble: shirt and bowtie included. The darkness made his golden skin, bright green eyes and hair in need of a trim stand out in tantalizing contrast.

"Keep looking at me like that," he murmured into her hair, "and I'll have to show you to one of the many private bedrooms."

She should scold him but couldn't. Finding a bedroom sounded, well…lovely.

The charity function was being held in the house's ballroom on the far east side—or as Pen liked to think of it, "left." They joined the well-dressed throngs clicking through the marble hallways and stopping to admire what had to be million-dollar-plus paintings and sculptures dotting the long corridor.

"Pretentious, right?" Zach muttered, earning a gasp from an older woman whose gray curls were piled on top of her head.

Pen swallowed the laugh pushing against her throat. If that older woman knew who Zach was would she be more or less offended?

It wasn't until they entered the ballroom where the silent auction was underway that the butterflies in Pen's tummy took flight. Right at the same moment her date said…

"There's my mom."

His mom. As in *a mom*. As in what Penelope would soon be—or was now, depending on when one started counting. She might start hyperventilating.

"Before I forget…" Zach stepped in her line of vision, taking it up with his fine attire and gorgeous self. "This is for you."

He reached into his pocket and light winked off a small metal object—okay, *now* she was going to hyperventilate.

He slid the band onto the third finger of Pen's left hand, a massive square-cut diamond in the center of an army of smaller diamonds. She…gaped. The ring was stunningly beautiful, and would likely require stronger biceps in order to hold her arm up while wearing it.

"Zach." Her gasp was muted, and then vanished altogether, when he lifted her knuckles and placed a kiss on them and the ring.

"Can't look engaged without the ring, now, can you?" His dimple made a brief appearance.

"I suppose not."

"Let's say hello." He offered his right arm and Pen looped her left hand around his elbow, trying hard not to stare at the blinding facets winking up at her.

"Eleanor Ferguson," he said when he reached his mother. "I have someone I'd like you to meet."

Eleanor turned, her martini balanced between manicured pink nails and a few stunning rings of her own, all diamond-encrusted and throwing off nearly as much light as Penelope's. Her blond hair was coiffed and stylish with warm honey highlights.

"Penelope, I presume."

Pen nodded.

"Please, call me Elle. It's wonderful to meet the woman who stole Zach's heart." There was nothing disingenuous about her smile, but Pen still felt as if the woman's reaction was a touch insincere.

"Heavens, Zach. Renaldo did well." Elle lifted Pen's left hand and examined the engagement ring. "Renaldo is our family jeweler. He's the best." She slid the pad of her thumb over the diamonds. "Perfect fit, too. A little wiggle room is always nice in case you eat too much salt."

Or if I'm pregnant with your grandchild.

"Where's Dad?"

"Hors d'oeuvres." Elle rolled eyes that were a muted shade of Zach's envious greens. "Since his heart attack, I make him eat healthy, but the very moment he's out of my sight, he's elbow deep in sausage canapés."

Elle waved over an extremely tall, white-haired man who was patting his lips with a napkin. Zach's father didn't look like a man who'd suffered a heart attack. He walked with a lazy swagger, his tuxedo fitted over his lean body. His hair tickled his collar, in need of a trim like his son's. His gray eyes narrowed on Penelope as he approached.

"Hey, son."

"Penelope Brand, this is my father, Rand, but everyone calls him Rider."

"Pretty girls like you can call me whatever you please," Rider said in a deep baritone before he kissed her hand. Then he held her hand out at arm's length.

"Congratulations on your engagement to Zach. Looks like he chose better the second time around."

"Rand! Honestly," Elle scolded, clucking her tongue. "It's lovely to meet you, Penelope. Zach, your brother was looking for you earlier. If you see him, do ask him to bring his date by to say hello. He's being quite rude."

Zach's parents linked arms and walked away and Penelope let out the breath going stale in her lungs.

"They're intense," she said.

"Are they?" Zach looked after them and then turned to face Penelope. "My mother's favorite phrase is *quite rude* by the way, so don't let that alarm you."

Still, the woman made Pen's shoulders crawl under her ears.

"What can I get you to drink?"

"Anything clear and sparkling." Sadly. She could use a glass of champagne.

"Club soda?"

"With a lime." What the hell. Might as well go crazy.

"Perfect timing. Stef!" Zach lifted his voice to be heard and a few heads turned in their direction. It was clear that he was comfortable in the stuffy crowd. Pen already wanted to slip outside for some fresh air.

"Hey, kids." Stefanie approached in a fuchsia dress, her dark blond hair wound into a fancy twist. She smiled over her martini. "Penelope, you have to try these. The gin is the best I've ever had."

"Pen's not drinking this evening. Hang out here for a moment with her while I get her a club soda."

"Club soda?" Stef asked, but her words bounced off Zach's retreating back.

"I haven't been feeling well today." It was the truth. Pen woke with morning sickness that kept her in bed an extra hour. She nibbled on saltine crackers while checking her email on her phone. She'd yet to throw up as a result of morning sickness, but she'd become increasingly grateful that her private office had an attached bathroom.

"You don't look the least bit pale, so that's a plus." Stefanie's assessing gaze trickled over her, and Pen worried for a moment the younger woman might see right through her facade.

"I hear your oldest brother has a date," Pen said, successfully rerouting Stef's gaze.

Stef's eyes swept the room. "He does. I met her. She's a stiff like he is."

Pen saw them then, a slight woman with dark hair whose arm was linked with Chase's. He was talking to his parents now, so there was no need to pass on Elle's observation that he was being *quite rude*.

"Did you bid on anything?" Pen asked Stef.

"The spa package." She pointed to one corner and then to a painting to the right. "And that horrible artwork."

A chuckle erupted out of Pen before she could help it.

"I like you, Penelope." Stef's sincerity was obvious. The woman didn't say things she didn't mean. Pen knew that much. "If anyone is going to enter this family, I'm glad it's you. Zach hasn't always had the best taste."

"Oh?" Pen stepped closer, curious about Zach's dating habits. "Let me guess. Complete playboy."

"He has a good heart, but most women never ac-

cess it. As for Yvonne and that Vegas wedding thing…
What the hell?"

"It is curious that he tied the knot with her." The
thin redhead seemed better suited for anyone other than
Zach Ferguson.

"He said getting married sounded fun," Stef said.
"But that's pretty much his prescription for life, isn't it?
If it sounds like a good time, why not attempt?"

Penelope's stomach sank. This time she did palm her
torso as a bout of queasiness overtook her.

What Stef said was true—and Pen had seen it in action. Zach introduced her as his fiancée the evening of
Chase's birthday party because it sounded fun. They
slept together that first night—and several nights there-
after because it was fun. Pen fell in line with that thinking because being around Zach made her embrace the
fun. His world was shimmering and enticing, and she'd
wanted some of that for herself.

Only that *fun* had turned into a baby due at the end of
this year. That *fun* had become a human being, half Zach,
half Pen. A baby wasn't something you "attempted"
because it sounded fun. There'd be no walking away if
their son or daughter suddenly lost his or her luster. At
least not for her. While she was definitely ill-equipped
for motherhood, she was willing to live and learn. Her
own mother had set a stellar example and, like her, Pen
planned on rocking the business world as well as a breast
pump. It'd take some practice and she was sure there
would be moments where she had no idea what she was
doing, but she'd manage.

What about Zach, though? Would her fake fiancé

turn his back on their child if he or she suddenly didn't fit into his *fun* lifestyle? Did Pen make a mistake letting him talk her into staying?

"Pen? You don't look so good." Stef's hand rested on Penelope's shoulder as the world swam in and out.

Pen's cheeks heated, her head spun and she rocked on her high heels. She swept her blurring vision over to Zach, who approached with a drink in each hand.

The last thing she remembered was him dropping both glasses to rush over as her world was swallowed in black.

Nine

Zach's concerned expression was the first sight Pen saw when she opened her eyes.

She reached for her forehead, where a damp weight sat, and pulled away a black washcloth.

He took it from her. "Stef, rewet this for me?"

His sister jumped to help, returning in a few seconds with a much cooler cloth. Zach pressed it to Pen's forehead again.

"No more high heels," he told her, a muscle flinching in his cheek.

"Leave her alone." Stef entered her range of vision again, this time with a water bottle. "Sip this, Pen."

Zach helped her sit up some and then Pen drank from the water bottle, her head much clearer than before. She'd been relocated to an enormous sitting room with settees and low coffee tables and several groupings of chairs. She looked down to find she was resting on a dove-gray chaise longue.

"You passed out. Did you eat today?" That was Zach, his voice low and angry, but his innate tenderness outlined every word.

"I ate a little," Pen mumbled, sitting up and putting her feet on the floor—her bare feet. "Where are my shoes?"

"I'll carry you to the limo. You're not putting those things on again." His mouth pulled down at the corners.

"Yes, I am. I can wear high heels as well as I can flats. Better, in fact."

"It's second nature after a while," Stef concurred. Then to Pen, she added, "He's being overly concerned."

"We need to check with the doctor." He stood from his kneeling position on the floor in front of her and sat on the edge of the lounger. "To make sure nothing's wrong."

"She's light-headed! There's nothing wrong." Stef rolled her eyes and took a bite out of what appeared to be a ham sandwich.

Pen's mouth watered. She literally licked her lips.

"Want half?" Stefanie offered a plate with the other half of her sandwich. "There was too much fancy food out there so I went to the kitchen and made a ham and cheese on white bread like a real American."

"I can get you anything you like from the caterer, Pen. You don't have to—" Zach started to argue.

"If you don't mind." She reached past him for the plate and Stef handed it over. Pen took one bite, then another, and in no time the half sandwich was demolished. "Thank you so much."

Zach took the plate. "Better?"

Pen slugged back the rest of the water and let out a satisfied *Mmm*. "Much better."

"Guess we forgot the eating for two part, didn't we?" He pushed a lock of hair away from her face before his eyes went wide at his faux pas.

"Oh my God! You guys are *pregnant*?" Stef stood from her seat on top of the coffee table, the remainder of her sandwich still in one hand. "I'm so excited! I'm going to be an aunt!"

"Stef," Zach growled. "We haven't told anyone yet."

His sister promptly returned her derrière to the coffee table and pressed her lips closed. She mimed zipping her lips but when she looked back to Pen, she air clapped.

"I'm going to take you home." Zach stood. "*My* home, where you'll be staying." He leveled Pen with an impatient glare before leaving the sitting room.

"Bossy." Stef polished off her sandwich and dusted her hands on her skirt like she was wearing jeans instead of Carolina Herrera.

"What does he mean 'where I'll be staying?'" she asked herself, but Stef answered.

"While you were unconscious, Zach said he was going to ask you to move in with him." Stef turned to study the doorway he'd disappeared through. "I guess that was his way of asking."

"You're overreacting," Penelope told Zach as he moved from the couch to the kitchen on Monday morning. She'd spent Saturday night at his house, and Sunday, too, but this was ridiculous. She was itching to go home. Despite him having stopped by her apartment to gather a few changes of clothes—and shoes—she was ready to sleep in her own bed. And, as of Monday morning, ready to work in her own office.

He returned to the living room with a steaming mug, a string and tag dangling from the edge.

"The doctor said plenty of fluids and that peppermint tea would help as long as you don't drink it too often." He placed the mug in front of her on the couch where he'd arranged a remote, a few paperback novels, magazines and a plate of cheese and crackers.

A doctor made a house call Saturday afternoon and told her everything seemed fine, though he'd like her to come in soon for an ultrasound. He did take her blood for a workup, so she was glad to have that unpleasantness over with.

Zach threw a blanket over her legs and Pen tossed it off with a laugh.

"It's nearly June, Zach. I don't need a blanket. I don't have the flu. I have morning sickness. I'm not going to sit here when I have work to do."

"Yes, you are."

"No. I'm not."

She stood and he took a step toward her. The room canted to one side and she gripped his biceps, willing her feet to keep her upright. Strong hands wrapped around her arms and when she looked sheepishly up at her caretaker, his eyes were filled with concern.

"Pen."

"Fine. I'll rest. But only for today. And I'm going to return emails, then maybe a few phone calls."

Sensing he'd lost the battle, Zach didn't argue. But then Penelope did make a show of sipping her tea and eating a cracker—no cheese yet; her stomach couldn't handle it.

"The doctor also said the nausea will subside. You won't feel like this every day." Zach, her new nursemaid, delivered a paper napkin to her next. She knew everything the doctor had said. She'd been there. But Zach was making her his top priority, and that was really…nice.

"Thank you." In all sincerity, she should be thanking him. He was overbearing and a worrywart, but he was also looking out for her. For a woman who'd been on her own since she started staying home alone at age eleven, Pen wasn't accustomed to someone taking care of her.

"I had lunch and dinner delivered. The meals are prepared and in the fridge. All you have to do is take the lid off and eat them."

When Zach started listing ingredients like "chicken salad on rye" Pen's stomach did a cannonball.

She held out a hand. "Don't say the word chicken or rye." She swallowed thickly. "Or salad."

He lowered to sit next to her on the sofa, cradling her face in his hands. "You're going to be okay here while I go to work?"

"Yes. Go." She gave him a halfhearted shove and he stole a kiss before standing. One more wave goodbye and he left.

She sat back on the couch and flipped on the TV, using the remote. She sipped her tea, kept down the crackers and yes, a few pieces of the mild Swiss cheese, and decided that maybe she could rest for a little while.

With her body being uncooperative, she could use the break.

Zach's mind was a million miles from work and the man currently droning on in front of him at the board meeting. He slid his gaze to his right where Armand jotted notes on his steno pad, and then to his left where Celia pecked notes into her iPad.

His mind was on Penelope and the scare she'd given him the night of the charity function at his parents' house.

He was able to play it off as her not feeling well to everyone except for Stefanie, thanks to his gaffe when he mentioned Penelope eating for two.

Since then, he'd been in productive mode. He'd taken Pen home, called the doctor and scheduled a house visit and made sure she had everything she needed at his place.

His cell phone buzzed and he grabbed on to the interruption like a lifeline. The entire meeting halted as he stood and checked the screen. Stefanie. Good enough for him.

"Continue without me. Celia, if you could email me your notes." With that, he was out the door, lifting his cell phone to his ear. "Zachary Ferguson."

"Oh, so formal. I like it."

"I have to keep up appearances for the suits."

"Aren't you one of them now?" He could hear her smile.

"Never say die, Stef. What's up with you?"

"I'm going to plan a bridal shower for your future wife," she answered, bringing him to a halt a few yards from his office door. "And I didn't know, if by the time I threw it, we'd also include the baby shower part. Thoughts?"

Woodenly, he moved to the sanctuary of his office and shut the door behind him. "No showers. We're doing this low-key."

"No low-key. You're a Ferguson and we do things very high-key. Or off-key, if we're talking about Dad's singing. I'm en route to the florist for a consultation for a fund-raiser dinner Mom is throwing, but I thought I'd ask about bridal arrangements while I was there. By the way, when is the wedding date?"

"We don't have a wedding date. No showers."

"Well, you'd better set one because that baby has a due date and I have a feeling he or she will stick to it whether you're married or not."

His face went cold as the blood drained from his cheeks. When he'd become "engaged" to Pen, no part of him believed they'd actually get married. Now that there was a baby on the way, well…he still hadn't planned on marrying her, but he also hadn't considered that everyone would expect them to make things official. Especially with a child who would carry on the Ferguson name.

"Have to run. Ciao!" Stefanie hung up on him and Zach set the cell phone on his calendar and stared dumbly at the month of May.

His sister had a point. Their baby was coming

whether or not he set a wedding date. If he and Pen didn't get married, in a few short weeks they'd have to announce a pregnancy and the decision not to wed.

It was archaic to believe they had to marry because they were expecting, but his parents would expect it. Especially now that they'd learned he'd married Yvonne on a whim.

Except no one knew the real reason for his marriage to Yvonne. It was a challenge in a way—to see if he could do it. Could he get over the past in one fell swoop without years of therapy or repression?

He could, as it turned out. He'd had to drink half the liquor in Nevada, but he'd walked down the aisle, had a spontaneous Vegas honeymoon and then wrapped things up in a matter of days.

All because once upon a time he'd been in love—for real. Yes, he'd been twenty-six, but he knew in his bones that Lonna was the one for him. She was four years older than him and had absolutely consumed every corner of his world.

They dated for a year and on that one-year anniversary when they sat across from each other at a rooftop bar, Zach proposed.

He recited a speech including how much he loved her, how there was no one else for him and how the rest of his life would be spent by her side.

Lonna had an announcement that evening, too. She'd come to break up with him. She'd had a speech prepared— it was about how she couldn't see herself with him past that year, and how she couldn't bring herself to lie to him because she didn't love him.

She'd said she never had.

It was a blow he was sure he'd never recover from. Thank God he'd kept the relationship quiet, only telling his parents and friends that they were "dating." After the breakup, he kept things quieter. He dodged questions, confided in no one and cried in private.

Then he decided he'd been humiliated for the last time, packed up his life and started a new one away from Dallas.

Now he had a decision to make. About a marriage. About a future with Penelope in his life.

No matter what those future plans entailed, one thing was certain: Pen and he might get married, they would have a baby, but Zach refused to allow himself to fall in love.

Not now.

Not ever again.

Ten

She wasn't sure what happened, but after a few hours of sipping tea and watching mindless daytime television, Penelope abandoned the vicinity of *craptastic* and exited the off-ramp of *amazing*.

She showered at Zach's house, dressed in her favorite pantsuit—white, of course—and slipped her feet into five-inch heels. She arrived at her office building via a town car—the number she'd pilfered from Zach's refrigerator—thanked the driver and stepped onto the downtown sidewalk.

It wasn't officially summer yet, but the Texas sun was hot. Judging by the passing professionals, summer was already here. Men had gone without their jackets, the women wore shorter hemlines and everyone, Pen included, had sunglasses perched on their noses.

She'd returned as many emails and phone calls as she could from her cell phone. She told herself that she was going to the office simply to retrieve her laptop, but now that she was here, she decided to stay. The idea of settling into her cushy desk chair, hands on the keyboard, was too tempting to resist.

Bonus, the embryo incubating in her uterus decided to allow her to keep the contents of her stomach. She'd be smart to take advantage of the reprieve.

Two hours into her routine, her planner boasted several checked-off boxes and lined-through tasks, and Pen's fingers were practically flying over the keys as she crafted an email to a reporter. Reporters and paparazzi were good friends to have when in PR. Even if they were less friends and more acquaintances with benefits.

She sent the email by punching the enter key with a flourish before standing to refill her water bottle. She'd pulled open her office door only a few inches when Zach rounded the corner, paper takeout bag in hand, a scowl on his face.

"Zach, hi!" Rather than fetch herself a much-needed drink, she pulled the door open the rest of the way and ushered him in. "How'd you know where to find me?"

"Tony told me."

The town car driver.

"Right. Well. Welcome to my humble office."

Zach didn't survey her digs, though. He set the paper bag on her desk and glowered down at her. "You're not at my house."

"Correct." She smiled.

"You didn't eat the food I left for you in the refrigerator."

At the mention of food, her stomach roared rather than wilted. That was a good sign—her appetite was back.

"I was going to order from the sandwich cart in the lobby." She'd been so wrapped up in work, she'd forgotten all about eating.

"Now you don't have to."

"Are you under the impression that I'm incapable of feeding myself?" She smiled sweetly.

"Don't be cute." His voice was thick with warning. "It's my responsibility to keep you in good health since this situation is at least half my doing."

"Ha! I'm not a prize pig, Zach. I'm responsible for myself. And I hope you're not suggesting that you need to ensure I eat for two because I'm neglecting our baby."

His brows slammed over his nose. "I'm not suggesting anything. I'm *telling* you that parenting, for me, starts here."

Her eyes went to the paper sack. That…was actually kind of sweet. Barbaric and completely chauvinist, but sweet. She hooked a finger on the edge of the bag and peeked inside. "You brought enough for both of us. Are you staying?"

Pen scraped the bottom of her salad bowl with the plastic fork to catch the last bit of honey mustard dressing and cranberry. She hummed while chewing, then opened her beautiful blue eyes and laid them right on

Zach. He was glad to see that the color had returned to her face.

"Thank you," she said. "This was delicious."

He raised the plastic container containing the remaining half of his Reuben sandwich, dripping with Thousand Island dressing and tart sauerkraut. "Want the rest of mine?"

Her eyes brightened. "Really?"

"Yes, really."

She eagerly accepted the container and wolfed down the rest of his sandwich. As she swiped her mouth with a napkin, he gathered the plastic containers and stuffed them into the paper sack so he could take them to the trash on the way out.

"Nice to have an appetite." She swallowed a few guzzles of water from the bottle he'd refilled for her. "It must kick in late afternoon."

The *bing* of her email inbox sounded again. That had to be the sixth or seventh time since they'd sat down to eat. She rose to check it and he rose with her, curling a hand around her slender wrist.

"It's after five, Pen. Time to clock off."

"Just let me check." She tilted her head, sending her blond hair sliding over breasts that were pushed against the low V-cut of her silky shirt.

Keeping her wrist captive, he lowered his lips to hers.

"No," he whispered, lifting his head to find her wearing a disdainful frown. "Gather your things and I'll drive you home."

"Oh, all right." She shut down her desktop computer and slid her laptop into a bag along with a few other files and her planner. "If you could send my things back to my place, I'd appreciate it. There are a few outfits I'd like to have on hand for this week."

"Home is my place, Penelope." He lifted the sack and her water bottle, holding the door open for her.

"No. I'm going to my house."

"Guess again. Let's go."

"Zach!" She straightened her back and squared her jaw, ready for a fight. He slid a lingering gaze down her body—over the fitted jacket and pants to the shoes he should have thrown out rather than hid in his closet.

He took a step closer to her and she adjusted the bag on her shoulder. "You're wearing the shoes I told you not to." His voice dipped to communicate his displeasure.

"It's a free country." She arched one fair eyebrow.

"You're coming to my house," he reiterated. He couldn't risk her slipping in the shoes or forgetting to eat or no one being there if she felt sick in the morning. He wanted her safe. He wanted her with him. "No more discussion."

"You can't keep me prisoner, you know." She propped a fist on one hip.

Stubborn thing…

Zach dropped the bag and scooped Pen against him, his arm locked at her lower back. He kissed her, his tongue plunging past her lips, pleased when her free hand went from pushing him away to fisting in his shirt and tugging him forward. A thrill pulsed through him when her lips went pliant and her tongue began sparring with his.

When she finally surfaced, he kissed her lips softly once, twice more, and made sure she was steady on her spindly shoes before letting her go.

He then bent and lifted the bag and smirked down at her. Her hair was rumpled, her jacket askance and her lips pink and swollen from his five o'clock shadow.

His. Through and through.

"Your place." She said it with an eye roll, and offered a droll, "But only because there's no one at my house who kisses me like that," over her shoulder while they walked to the elevator.

Yeah, he thought she'd see things his way.

"Engaged?" Penelope's mother squawked into the phone.

Penelope'd had a feeling the news would be a surprise. Her mother knew Pen had all but sworn off men since one ran her out of Chicago.

Paula Brand had always been a busy woman. When Penelope was growing up, one indelible fact stood out about her mother: she worked.

Part of Pen's work ethic had come directly from her mother. Yes, her father worked on their co-owned real estate business, but it was Paula whom Penelope had always wanted to grow up and be like.

"I'm getting you the news a little late," Pen said. "There was a bit of a kerfuffle here in Dallas about my being engaged to the mayor's brother." Not that the news would have traveled to Chicago.

"Well, what's he like? Other than being the mayor's brother," her mother said, rustling papers. Paula was most likely sitting at the kitchen table of her latest project. Pen could imagine a paper-strewn surface surrounded by refinished cabinet drawers leaning against every wall, stacks of to-be-installed tile dotting worn linoleum. Paula was usually busy with one house project or the next, but she always made time for her only daughter.

"Well, I actually met him in Chicago in passing a few years back." Hopefully this would foster the notion that she hadn't rushed into anything. "He relocated to Dallas, and when I did, too, I ran into him at…a concert." Concert seemed better than a club. No way was Pen sharing what transpired that evening. Namely: the conception of their son or daughter.

"What does the mayor's brother *do*?" Possibly the most important question her mother could've asked. Vocation in the Brand family was paramount. The answer would please her, Pen was sure.

"He's the CEO of Ferguson Oil."

A drawn out silence, and then, "Impressive." Her mother took a breath and then issued a warning of sorts. "I hope this man has more to him than money. I raised you to support yourself."

Paula, though in a strong marriage with Pen's father, had always encouraged her to be independent. She knew her mother was looking out for her rather than accusing her of chasing a man because of the size of his wallet.

"Funny story. I didn't even know about his monetary status until we became serious. He used to be a contractor. A very good one. He came home to run the family business."

"Even when you try to go blue-collar, you end up

with a suit." Paula's tone was filled with mild humor, yet approving. "That sounds like you."

Zach looked as delicious in worn jeans as he did in suits, if memory served. Pen hadn't had much of an opportunity to see him in jeans—though he had worn a pair of low-slung sweats the other night that nearly made her eyes tumble from their sockets. This morning he'd kissed her while she slept, and walked out of the bedroom wearing his running gear. She regretted now not waking up completely to take in the view.

"If you are happy, darling, I'm happy," her mother said. "That's all I want."

"Thanks, Mom." Her support would make the baby bombshell easier to drop in the future.

"As long as this man is ten times the man Cliff was."

Unfortunately, Pen hadn't been able to hide the circumstance that drove her out of Chicago and away from her parents. When she'd decided to relocate to Dallas, she'd told them the truth.

"Zach is one hundred times the man Cliff was." She'd been pacing the living room as she talked on her cell phone, so when she turned on her heel to pace back, she was surprised to find the subject of her conversation already in the room. She bid her mother farewell, and with a promise to check in soon, ended the call.

"I can get used to coming home to high compliments." Zach's words were puffed out between a few labored breaths. "You're up."

"Did you take the stairs?" Not what she wanted to say, but she had to fill the gap of silence that had mostly involved her staring. Zach's black T-shirt was damp with sweat, his biceps pressing the edges of the sleeves, and his strong legs poking out from beneath a pair of gray shorts. Had she ever known a man with a body this incredible? She didn't have to think long to come up with that answer.

No. No was the answer.

"I confessed to my mother about the engagement. I figured if she was comfortable with the idea of us getting married, she'll embrace the idea of being a grandmother."

He nodded, taking the information in stride. "Guess we should make that announcement eventually. I'm not sure how long we can hide it."

She dragged her palm over her flat stomach. She wasn't showing yet, but she would be soon enough.

"We could always tell everyone we were waiting until we were positive nothing would go wrong."

"It's our news to share whenever we want, for whatever reasons we decide."

She liked Zach's confidence. She liked sharing this with him. Though unexpected, the baby was their little secret—well, theirs and Stef's.

"I'm going to grab a shower. Join me?" His crooked smile went a long way to convincing her to do just that. Unfortunately...

"I already took one. And I have another phone call to make. Rain check?"

Even sweaty, he was sexy. He strolled over, water bottle in hand, and grinned down at her. The earthy outdoor scent wafting off him didn't deter her in the least—only made her want him more.

"In your case, Penelope, it's always raining."

The delicious lilt of his drawl was enough to bring her to her tiptoes. She placed a kiss on his lips and when he pulled back he dragged his top teeth along his full bottom lip. That move almost made her change her mind.

Almost.

Her mother's words echoed in her mind. Penelope had been raised to support herself.

Sexy baby daddy or no, her workday called.

Eleven

Serena Fern and Ashton Weaver sat at a round table by the swimming pool, Pen across from them in a matching cushioned wicker chair. She'd met them at Ashton's mansion, per his request, and was as grateful for the peppermint candy he offered as much as the warmth of the summer sun.

These two were currently interviewing for a public relations specialist to handle an incident that happened during a particularly wild party where Serena, who was engaged to Michael Guff, her manager, was photographed sliding lips with her fellow actor, Ashton.

And who could blame her? Serena and Ashton were in their early twenties and Michael was pushing forty.

In their matching aviator sunglasses, Serena and Ashton looked very much like a couple. Especially since they held hands on the tabletop next to three sweating glasses of lemonade.

"We want to go public," Ashton declared. "She doesn't love Michael."

Serena's smile was sweet—hopeful. She liked that Ashton claimed her; Pen could tell that much.

"You *are* public," Pen informed them. "You're public in a big way." TMZ had plastered those photos all over the internet. There was nothing demure about Serena in her string bikini in this very pool and Ashton's tongue visible as she clung to his neck. The engagement was off, but Serena said Michael hadn't dropped her as a client yet. Because he was smart. He knew Serena was at the top of her game, and wasn't about to let his cash cow go. So to speak.

"I don't want to be the bad guy here. I look like I cheated." Serena's full pout appeared. She was gorgeous, if not a petite little thing.

"You *did* cheat," Pen reminded her. Her clients came to her for the truth and she wasn't holding back. "The good news is, most of the public will see this as predatory. Michael knows what he's doing. He wooed you with his professionalism and expertise. We'll perpetuate the story that he was marrying you for a cut of your money. A few timely interviews and tweets, and then you and Ashton can go public. For now, you can be seen together, but no kissing. No hand-holding. Go out and have coffee—better yet, with your scripts like you're rehearsing. In a few weeks you can snog in public all you like."

Serena grinned. Ashton didn't.

"What about Michael?"

Pen smiled. And here came the part where the young actors hired her.

"I'd recommend Serena firing him."

Ashton grinned. Serena gasped.

"Can I...do that?" she asked.

"Not only can you do that, you should. I know a couple of wonderful agents who could recommend someone reputable for your career."

"And then we could stop sneaking around and pretending it was an accident." Serena grasped Ashton's hands with both of hers and then, the two most adorable people ever embraced and kissed in a way that made Pen uncomfortable.

Job acquired, Pen left Ashton's mansion and those two to their inevitable lovemaking. Serena's words wound around her brain as Pen climbed into her car. *Sneaking around.*

While Pen and Zach weren't exactly sneaking, it irked her that she didn't have a blueprint for their situation. This was what she did for a living—she should be able to draw up a concise plan.

Which would be...what?

She thought back to Chicago, to Reese and Merina Crane's marriage of convenience, and how it turned into love despite starting as a farce.

Is that what Pen was hoping would happen with her and Zach? Because that was...silly.

What they had was an engagement that had started out as a distraction for Zach's PR issue. What they cur-

rently had was an entanglement that couldn't be resolved by a few tweets and sound bites.

What they had was a budding family and Pen
needed to decide how, exactly, to move forward while
preserving the Ferguson family's good name.

She drove to her apartment, deep in thought about
what that plan would look like. How she and Zach
would maintain a friendship throughout raising their
child. When the best time would be to announce the
dissolving of their engagement.

Probably the wisest move was to announce the baby
on the heels of them not being engaged—that way
everyone would be too excited about the baby to focus
on the breakup.

Sigh.

Maybe she should hire a PR person to handle her
case.

From where she sat, everything looked muddy.

At her apartment, she pulled into the lot. Without
a private garage like Zach had, she didn't have much
choice but to park her car in the elements. As luxurious
as his apartment and amenities were, she couldn't stay
there forever. She had to start thinking about where to
put the baby—and considering that her apartment was a
compact one-bedroom, one-bath, that meant she would
have to consider moving.

Perhaps that was the first order of business.

She stepped from her car and turned for the property
manager's office directly across from her building. As
luck would have it, Jenny was heading her way.

"Ms. Brand." Her cropped blond hair blew in the

summer breeze. She wore a fitted pencil skirt and a button-down shirt over a pair of sensible pumps. "Great timing. I was coming to give you this."

"Oh?" Pen pushed her hair behind her ear and accepted the paper Jenny offered. "What is it?"

"Your lease has been terminated. Congratulations on your engagement!" Jenny squeezed Pen's upper arm. "I hate to see you go, but I'm thrilled you've found love. Zach told me it was a surprise—his wedding gift to you. *Ohmygoshisthatthering?*" She snatched Pen's left hand and admired the diamond resting there, before rerouting her hand to her chest. Pen swore the other woman was tearing up. "You have until the end of the month to clear your things. No hurry, but honestly, I wouldn't hesitate moving in with a man who gives you a rock like this one!"

Before she could respond to…well, any of it, Jenny waved and said something about returning to her desk. Pen watched her go, the paper in her hand blowing and folding in half. She straightened it and read over the words Paid In Full as her temper skyrocketed.

Yes, she'd been contemplating moving from her one-bedroom into a larger place, but she wasn't planning on moving in with Zach.

She lifted her cell phone and punched in his number. When he answered in his office-y voice, she let him have it.

"I'm homeless." She wrestled her keys from her bag and marched inside her building.

"You're far from homeless," came his easy response.

"I'm not moving into your apartment, Zach."

"No. You're not."

She blinked as she pushed the button on the elevator for her floor. "Pardon?"

"I'm looking at a house right now. There's not enough room for a baby at my place." His voice sounded distant when he spoke to someone other than her. "I'll take it."

"Zach?"

"Gotta go, gorgeous. I have paperwork to deal with."

"Zach."

But one glance at her cell phone and she could see he'd already ended the call.

Zach tried Pen's phone number again only to be greeted by voice mail. He tapped the screen on the dashboard to end the call and pulled off the highway, changing direction to drive to her apartment. If she wasn't there, he'd try her office, and if she wasn't *there*, he'd see her at his apartment tonight.

When he'd gone to her place of residence to pick up a few things for her a week ago, he'd nearly had an aneurysm. The apartment building was in need of more than paint and TLC, and the area wasn't the safest. He'd decided then and there to keep her close by. Safe. Now that she was having his baby, there was no need for her to struggle.

He didn't want their child growing up worried about his or her safety.

From what he could tell, Pen dumped all her money into her office. He understood why. With a job like hers, working with business and celebrity elite, she needed to look the part.

He drove through the parking lot but there was no sign of Pen's car. He'd try her office next. He hit the screen on his dashboard to call her cell again, knowing it was futile.

But then her voice surprised him.

"I'm trying to be mad at you."

He couldn't help smiling. Not because she was mad at him but because hearing her voice lined with anger meant she was safe. She was okay.

"Where are you?"

"Why? Planning on coming by and buying me out of whatever building I'm in? What if I'm shopping?"

"A shopping center is well within my pay grade."

Her silence let him know his joke didn't fly.

"I want to know where you are so I can show you our new house."

"Zach."

"We also need to talk about our plans and what we're sharing when. I'm not going to dodge questions when they start rolling in, regardless of my brother's political career or Ferguson Oil's reputation. I'm not going to hide you or what we're doing."

"I agree. We need a plan." Her voice was wooden, but he'd take the agreement. "I don't want that, either."

"All right, then. Where are you? I'll take you to dinner."

"I'm at your apartment. Throwing your clothes out the window." Her voice was petulant, but he could guess she was kidding.

"I guess I have to buy that shopping center after all."

More silence.

"Pen."

"Come home. We'll talk then."

The way she said *home*, with ownership, and invited him to join her, snagged his chest.

"I was serious about dinner," he said as he sat back in his seat and accelerated.

"You bet your sweet ass you are," Pen snapped. "I'll see you soon."

Another grin. Damn, he liked her feisty.

He liked her, period.

At home he found Penelope dressed down in a tight pair of form-fitting pants and a baggy tee. Her hair was in a ponytail and she was on the floor, eyes closed, hands resting on her knees.

"Yoga?" he guessed, setting his cell phone and brief-case on the kitchen counter.

"I'm meditating so I don't kill you," she said without opening her eyes. Then she did, and pegged him with a pair of pale blues that never failed to make him smile. She had a pull on him—a physical one, sure, but there was a deeper connection there. Because of the baby? Yes, that was definitely part of it, but that wasn't all. "How was your day, dear?"

"Hectic. I bought a house."

"I heard." Her mouth flattened. She reached behind her and lifted a sheet of paper, waving it in the air for him. "I lost mine."

"I wanted it to be a surprise."

She stood from her mat and slapped the paper against his chest. "I was surprised."

He palmed the paper and followed her into the

kitchen. She swallowed a few drinks of water before gesturing to the paper he still held. "Flip it over."

Her handwriting took up the entire backside of the page.

"'PR Plan for Zachary Ferguson and Penelope Brand,'" he read.

"I drafted our plan."

Under their names were dates and bulletpoints for items like "announce end of engagement" and "be seen shopping for baby" and "press release."

"This is…interesting." He couldn't come up with another word for it.

"This is the way we're doing it."

"I don't see a line item for moving into my house."

"Sorry. I'm going to be living apart from you before that happens." She waggled her hand where the engagement ring sat. "The breakup and all."

"I don't see why we have to break up." He felt his brow furrow while hers lifted.

"Because this isn't real. I've orchestrated engagements before. I've even dealt with unplanned pregnancies. Couples don't usually argue with my sound and reliable suggestion to announce a split." She bit her lip. "Mostly."

Mostly.

He wondered if that meant some of the couples she'd walked through the valley of the shadow of matrimony fell in love for real and unraveled her precious plans. That wasn't their case, but he could see the discomfort in her expression.

He set the paper aside and walked toward her until

she plastered her back against the fridge and lifted her chin to take him in. There wasn't anything quite like her delicate features contrasted with all that strength and sass. She was a drug.

His palm on her stomach, he crowded her until his body was pressed against hers. "*This*. Is real."

"I know," she said just above a whisper. "But the engagement isn't."

"There's no reason to dismantle it yet. We could say we're waiting to marry until after you have the baby."

She gave him a slow nod, her eyes averting. "Is that what you want?"

Yes. Because he knew what he didn't want. He didn't want her to leave. He didn't want to miss a single moment of the pregnancy. That was only one of the reasons he wanted her to move in. He wanted to watch over her, but he also wanted to be with her.

"How about this for a proposal?" he asked, pleased when she turned her head, and her lips were dangerously close to his. "Move into my house. Have my baby. Wear this ring."

"And then what?"

"We have time to decide the *what*, Penelope." He palmed her soft cheek and ran his thumb over her bottom lip. "In the meantime, I want you in my house. In my bed. In my world."

"You don't have to—"

"Let me. Allow yourself to let me. You don't have to have a rigid plan for your own life, Pen. Live on the edge." He gave her a lazy grin. "It's fun here."

She licked her lips and before she could argue, he

covered them with a kiss. Deflecting? Possibly. Where they were concerned, there was one surefire way to get them back on track and that was in the bedroom.

"You promised me dinner," she breathed, but her fists clung to him.

He was aware of the time, more aware of her pending hunger than his hardening manhood. "Are you hungry?"

"Starving." Her eyebrows bent in the sincerest apology. "How about after dinner?"

"You have to ask?" He shook his head, still marveling over how off-kilter this woman could throw him. "Dinner. Get changed."

Her beaming smile made him almost as happy as having her underneath him. She bounced out of the kitchen and down the hallway and Zach took another look at the paper in front of him.

He grabbed a pen from a nearby drawer and drew a line through "announce end of engagement."

Twelve

Having billions of dollars made moving much easier.

When Pen moved, she'd hired movers and packed every one of her belongings, plus loaded many of the boxes into her own car, for the traverse to Dallas from Chicago.

When Zach moved, he made one phone call to an assistant to gather Penelope's belongings from her apartment, and another to an interior designer to decorate his new home.

Two weeks had passed since the move from her apartment. His buying her out of her lease was heavy-handed, but she could admit it made sense in the short-term. Everyone would assume it was the natural next step after hearing about the pregnancy. Plus, Zach would need more room for the baby whether Pen lived with him or not.

He'd purchased a beautiful home just outside the city,

with six bedrooms and six bathrooms and a sprawling yard. A low stone wall ran the perimeter of the property, and the front featured a gate, not unlike Chase's mansion.

The house was far more approachable than a mansion, however, with a wide front porch and white columns, and, thanks to a savvy interior decorator, a pair of rockers on the porch overlooking the front yard and curved driveway.

That was where she and Zach sat tonight.

She'd finished up at work and he'd met her at home for dinner—a dinner cooked by a chef he'd hired to monitor her feedings, or so she'd joked. Now they sat, a mug of peppermint tea for her, and a cold beer for him, rocking back and forth on the porch.

"This is really beautiful, Zach."

He turned his head and smiled. Tonight he wore jeans and a T-shirt, looking the part of laid-back country boy. Even the recent trim of his hair couldn't dash the relaxed line of his long body. He pushed, one knee crooked, the other leg straight out, and rocked again, finishing his bottle of beer before setting it on the wooden porch.

"Glad you like it."

She tapped her mug with her fingernails and thought. The PR plan for them had been drawn up. She'd typed it neatly, presented it to him and he'd made changes—some she'd agreed to, others she hadn't.

Maintain engagement (to be revisited after the baby is born)

Shopping for the baby (covered by the press)

Press release confirming baby Ferguson

"We should talk," she said.

Zach's hands gripped the arms of the rocker and he slowly turned to face her. His eyebrows were down, his mouth flat.

"It's not bad!" she assured him with a soft laugh.

"Do me the favor of never saying those three words to me again?" He visibly relaxed some, sucking in a deep breath.

There had to be a story behind his request, but she wasn't going into that now.

"It's time to tell our families." She placed her hand over her tummy. She'd always had a slim waist, but the bump was showing enough that people would start talking. "I can't hide this much longer. And I'd like to tell them before we're seen at the store."

"That'd be best, yes." His ease returned, along with his smile.

"How about this weekend? We can stop by your parents' house before going to Love & Tumble." The upscale boutique selling children's clothing was bordering pretentious, but for the press release, they needed the attention. What better store to emerge from carrying several shiny sage-green bags in their hands while kissing? She'd already lined up a photographer and requested the shots.

"And your parents?"

"We can't very well fly to Chicago, now can we?"

"Why not?" He shrugged. "It's a two-hour flight."

"On your private jet?" She snorted. This amount of convenience was all so…hard to get used to.

"I don't own one, but I can charter a plane." He leaned on one arm, coming closer to her chair. "Your parents might want to meet me."

She nodded, her fantasy world ripping at the seams. Once her parents met him, once he was on her stomping grounds, would the fantasy bubble burst? She'd been sheltered, in a way. Living in this safe existence with work and Zach. Sequestered from reality while she juggled nausea, fatigue and doctor's appointments.

"I'll book it for Friday. We can grab a hotel."

A dry laugh chafed her throat. "My parents would die if we booked a hotel. They would insist we stay with them."

"We can stay with them."

She watched him for a solid beat, wondering who this man was, really. Was he the billionaire who moved them into a regal house with the snap of his fingers? Or the family guy kicked back on a rocking chair? Could he be both?

"Friday," she repeated, still unsure.

He grabbed his empty beer bottle, stood from the rocker and bent to kiss her. "But we're still having sex at your parents' house, whether they like it or not."

She pressed a hand to her cheek as he walked inside, waiting until he'd gone to react. Despite her worries about Friday—when reality met fantasy—Zach's comment made her laugh.

"How perfect that you both made it here for Fourth of July weekend!" Paula Brand grinned as she piled raw seasoned steaks and chicken breasts onto a platter.

Penelope's father, Louis, came in from the back and accepted the platter, slicing Zach in two with a curt nod.

Zach was accustomed to suspicious reactions from fathers of the women he'd dated—he'd met a few. Mothers loved him but the dads were harder to win over. Zach took a healthy slug from his beer bottle. He just had to come up with the how.

He'd played down the "Dallas billionaire" bit, sliding into his clothing from his Chicago days. A comfortable and approachable pair of jeans paired with a gray T-shirt.

Penelope opted for a billowy summer dress, cut to disguise the roundness of her belly starting to make itself known. She was leaning against the counter, a carbon copy of her mother, with an hourglass figure and blond hair. Paula's blond was a paler shade, her stature shorter, but she was as womanly and beautiful as her daughter.

A vision of Pen at that age, standing over a sink while Zach flipped through the mail hit him square in the solar plexus. His next breath was a struggle, but he managed.

"Zach, honey?"

He blinked out of his fortune-seeing stupor to find Paula's brows lifted in question.

"Another beer?"

"Oh. Sure. Yeah. Thanks."

Pen raised an eyebrow in his direction but moved to the fridge on his behalf. When she handed over the bottle, she smiled up at him, her eyes sparkling and skin glowing.

It seemed no matter how he tried to cordon off this situation as one he could control, she continually kicked down barriers and knocked him off center.

The real kicker? He didn't mind it a bit.

"Pen tells me you were a contractor when you lived here," Paula said as Zach took a swig of his fresh beer. "What do you think of this place?"

Paula and Louis bought and sold real estate for a living, so their current digs was a three-bed, two-bath fixer-upper north of Chicago.

"Good bones," he said, happy to turn his attention to the surrounding rooms. They'd obviously moved in here while they did the work. The house was clean, but there were various projects started in the kitchen, one of the bedrooms, and the half-bath downstairs had been gutted.

"We bought it for a steal." Paula washed the cutting board and her hands. "Foreclosure. We're hoping to double our profit. Louis insists on rebuilding the back deck, but I wanted to tear it down."

"The deck is a good feature." Zach walked to the back door. Louis manned the grill, his stout, muscular body stiff. The deck was worn and splintered, and a pile of fresh wood was lying under a tarp in the backyard.

Maybe after they told Pen's parents about the baby, and Louis *didn't* murder him and bury his body in the backyard, Zach and Pen's father would have a topic in common.

Zach knew how to build a deck.

Pen didn't miss the wind in the windy city, that was for sure. She'd wrestled her hair into a ponytail and was forced to hold her paper plate down with one hand while she ate her chicken sandwich to keep it from blowing away.

Her parents' temporary deck, strewn with Craftsman

tools, made her feel right at home. She remembered many occasions where she'd sidestepped piles of wood or stacks of tile in whatever house they were currently working on. After she moved out, they'd started moving into the homes they were flipping. She was glad they'd waited because as much as the nomadic lifestyle appealed to her hardworking family, Pen liked to be in one place. It was what had made leaving Chicago so difficult.

Her mother peppered Zach with questions about his family and his job, which he handled with ease as he sawed into his second steak. Pen's father did a good job of shoving food in his mouth whenever her mom tried to include him in the conversation, so that all he had to do was nod or shake his head in response.

Pen pushed her sandwich aside, focusing on the potato salad on her plate. She waited for a lull in the conversation and when it came she reached under the picnic table and grabbed Zach's knee. He jerked his attention toward her, gave her a subtle nod and put down his cutlery.

"Mr. and Mrs. Brand," he started, and Pen's stomach flopped. She hoped her dinner stayed down.

Paula looked up, eyebrows aloft and Louis did his impersonation of Sam the Eagle from *The Muppets*. Seriously. If his eyebrows were any lower they'd be his mustache.

"Pen and I have an ulterior motive for visiting this weekend, other than showing off the engagement ring."

Miraculously, her father managed to lower his eyebrows farther.

"We're excited to tell you that—" Zach put an arm around Pen and hugged her close, looking down into her eyes when he made the announcement "—we're expecting a baby in December." He faced her parents first, then Pen followed suit, in time to witness their twin expressions of shock.

"I beg your pardon?" That was her mom, who, knife and fork in hand over her plate, sat statue-still while the wind whipped her hair.

"We're pregnant, Mom. You and Dad are going to be grandparents."

"Oh, my. I'm…" Her mouth froze open until finally, *finally*, that gape turned into a wide smile. "I'm so happy!" She was off her chair so fast to wrap her arms around Pen's neck that Louis had to slap his hand down on her plate to keep it from blowing off the table.

Paula returned to her seat, chattering about due dates and how she'd have to apply for a credit card that offered frequent flier miles so she could visit Dallas on a regular basis.

"No need, Mrs. Brand," Zach said smoothly. "We'll fly you down."

At the kind offer, Louis stood with his plate and climbed over the picnic bench's seat. He grunted once, then stormed into the house, letting the screen door bang behind him.

That went about like Pen had expected.

Thirteen

"They're okay." Paula was peeking out of the kitchen window overlooking the deck.

"You mean Dad isn't strangling Zach or freezing him out completely?"

"Nope." Paula returned to the living room with two mugs of tea. "They're measuring."

"Measuring…do I want to ask what?"

"The deck, sweetheart." Paula handed over a mug.

"Oh, that."

Her mother sat on the dilapidated couch next to her, placing a comforting hand on Pen's knee. "This seems very sudden."

"Three months is one quarter of the year. It's not that sudden." Pen held her tea close to her lips. She hadn't meant to sound so defensive.

"Three months is how long you've been pregnant. When did you meet him?"

"I told you. When I lived here. That's been years ago." Pen lifted her thumbnail and nibbled. Her mother's serious expression remained. "Yes. Okay, it was sudden."

"But you're in love."

Thank goodness her mother didn't put a question mark at the end of that sentence. Pen didn't like to lie. She smiled instead. No, she and Zach weren't in love. What they had wasn't ever supposed to be about love. She couldn't deny she felt close to him—and that she liked him a whole lot.

When she thought of her baby, a worrisome thought niggled its way forward. Would her son or daughter grow up thinking love was a fairy tale?

No, she decided in an instant.

Pen would show her child love, and Zach would, too. Romantic love was avoidable. She thought back through her past boyfriends and wasn't sure she'd ever been in love herself. There'd always been an obstacle, an excuse she'd found to keep from getting in too deep.

Maybe because she'd arranged many false marriages and engagements for publicity and had become the ultimate skeptic. Or maybe the idea of giving in and being someone's all meant she'd be at risk to lose it all.

With a child on the way, she couldn't afford to be selfish.

A pair of low male laughs carried on the Chicago wind and into the living room and Penelope and Paula exchanged glances.

"Are they…?" Pen started.

Paula blinked, then smiled. "I think they are."

Zach and Pen's baby would know love—so much of it, he or she would never want for more.

But as she made that empty assurance to herself Pen wondered if she could settle for the same.

Louis not only liked to talk about houses and building, he was also a Dallas Cowboys fan.

Go fucking figure.

Zach ended up at the picnic table drinking beers and yapping with Pen's father until well after midnight.

"I should go up," Louis said. He cast a glance at an upstairs window. "Paula waits for me."

How…nice. Zach's parents got along fine, but he didn't remember his mother ever waiting on his dad, or his dad cutting anything short to go to her.

Louis stood and Zach stood with him. "Thanks for letting us stay."

"Paula insisted on always having a guest room for Pen since she moved to Dallas. We lost her to Texas a year before we're losing her to you." Louis's words held no venom, and actually sounded kind of sad. "You'll see when that baby is born. Just how much you'll do for it. Just how protective you'll become."

Zach could imagine. He'd already been that way with Penelope. He met Louis's eyes and confessed just that.

"I'm like that about your daughter. She'll never want for anything. Our child wasn't the reason we became engaged." His ex-wife was, but Zach sure as hell wasn't sharing that. "But the baby definitely gave us a good reason to stay that way."

Louis nodded slowly, obviously trying to accept the fact that his baby girl had gotten engaged and impregnated by some billionaire cowboy. Damn if Zach could understand Pen's father's position when he imagined having a daughter of his own.

With a slap to Zach's shoulder, Louis echoed his fear. "God help you if you have a girl."

Zach shut the door to the guest bedroom after brushing his teeth, stepping lightly across the real wood floors that were scarred and in need of a good wax. Paula had mentioned as much when she'd shown them to their room before looking to Zach to check if he'd be appalled by staying in such squalor. Her words, said on a tight laugh.

He'd assured her he could sleep anywhere, and though he'd kept it to himself, he'd also considered that he *would* sleep anywhere as long as Penelope was by his side.

He climbed into the double bed, a tight fit, the mattress sagging in the center. Pen let out a soft hum and wiggled under the blankets. Wrapping his arm around her middle, he tugged her close and buried his nose in her hair.

When he'd met her years ago in Chicago at a party, he'd been in full-on playboy mode. He'd set his Dallas drawl to full-tilt and laid on the charm, promising not to get into any trouble lest Pen's PR firm would have to step in and straighten him out. He hadn't seen her after that, so running into her at a swanky club in Texas had taken him by surprise.

He wasn't a man who believed in fate, kismet or meant-to-be, but as he allowed his fingers to drape over his fiancée's abdomen, he wondered if he wasn't seeing this for what it was.

A second chance.

But as the thought hit him, so did the palpable fear of screwing it up. Of being in a position to lose not only the woman beside him but also access to their child.

Zach hadn't thought about fatherhood. Hadn't thought about it even when he'd asked Lonna to marry him. But the moment Pen announced her pregnancy an overwhelming feeling of right swept over him.

It wasn't just the baby. It wasn't just that he was in his thirties and it was past time for him to consider starting a family. It wasn't that he'd crafted a fake engagement to distract from the real issue at hand.

The game-changer was Penelope Brand.

She murmured in her sleep—or her half sleep, as it were—and he kissed her shoulder. He'd promised to claim her in this very bed, parents' house or no, believing their sexual chemistry would rival the need for sleep and trump the need to be quiet with her parents down the hall.

Now, though…

She rolled in his direction, her eyes opening briefly then shutting again. The moonlight streamed through the window, highlighting her fair hair and kissing her curved cheekbone.

He'd claim her in a different way tonight.

He scooted in the springy bed to give her room. Her body was going through the rigorous toils of crafting a baby—their baby—and she needed all the sleep she could get.

He couldn't give her everything, but that, he could.

The flight home from Chicago was quick, and soon enough Zach and Pen were changing from their comfy flight clothes into slightly more formalwear for visiting the Ferguson house.

One set of parents down, one to go.

She'd let Zach choose the nature of the venue, which he'd scheduled for cocktail hour. She'd argued about building their visit around alcohol since she wouldn't be having any but he'd assured her she didn't have to worry.

At a little after seven Saturday evening, Pen settled onto the settee across from the chaise longue in the sitting room at the Ferguson mansion.

Elle was perched formally on the edge of a high-backed chair, Rider settled into the one next to it. A female member of the house staff walked in with a tray holding four martinis with speared olives in each elegant glass.

Zach accepted his glass, but held up a hand when the younger woman bent to give Penelope her drink. "My fiancée is expecting, so she'll need something non-alcoholic. Club soda with a lime, okay?" He pegged Pen with a playful look while she struggled not to swallow her tongue.

Evidently, breaking the news to his parents wasn't going to be a slow build.

Rider accepted his drink, Elle hers, and Pen offered

a shaky smile in response. Elle's right eyebrow was curved so high on her forehead, it'd been lost in her hair.

No one said a word until Pen had a club soda in hand. Elle went first.

"And here we thought you'd come to tell us that your engagement was a sham to distract from your ex-wife."

"Eleanor, for the love of—" Rider let out an exasperated huff and swallowed a mouthful of his martini.

"You're only allowed one of those, don't forget. Savor it."

Pen stiffened, but the comforting weight of Zach's arm was around her back in an instant.

"We're due in December. We wanted to tell you in person before you found out from someone else."

Elle pursed her already pursed lips, her cool green stare assessing and, from Pen's vantage point, not all that approving.

"I think it's great," Rider said with a huge smile. Pen latched on to the man's sentiment like a lifeline. "We already wrote you a check." He reached into the pocket of his slacks and came out with a folded paper. "It's for the wedding, but now I suppose you can include it with preparing for our first grandchild."

He let out a hearty laugh and embraced Elle's hand. "Better than croaking of a heart attack before I get to meet my grandkids, eh, Elle?"

"I suppose that's true." She narrowed her eyes again and Pen shifted in her seat. "What interested you most in my son, Ms. Brand? His money or his DNA?"

Next to her, Zach went on alert, but Pen stayed his retort by touching his arm.

"I can understand how this information comes as a shock to you, but there's no need to be rude, Mrs. Ferguson. I'm neither a gold digger nor a woman who expected to get pregnant. Trust me when I tell you that you don't want to know the part of your son that most interests me. I simply saw someone I liked." She paused to take in Zach, whose mouth flinched like he might be fighting a proud smile. "And had to have him."

She snapped her attention back to Elle, who'd dropped her jaw. Likely no one dared speak to the Oil Queen of Dallas the way Pen had, but the older woman had started it.

"Mom."

Elle turned her stunned reaction to Zach.

"We're not asking your permission, or for your approval. But I expect you to be much more gracious when the baby is here. He or she will be the first-born grandchild in the family."

Elle drank down her martini in hearty gulps, then retrieved the spare martini left behind when Pen refused it and gulped that one, too.

Rider, his good humor intact, let out a crack of laughter. "Guess she'll be having my second one, then."

Fourteen

"Pen, hang on."

The moment they'd exited Zach's parents' house, Pen marched down the driveway, fists at her sides.

"Wait." Zach caught her easily, snagging her biceps with a gentle hand and spinning her to face him. He was grinning and she glared at the dimple rather than admire it. Nothing about this evening had been funny.

"They hate me."

"No, they don't."

"Your mother hates me."

"No, she doesn't. She's just…in shock. Not everyone is going to take this news as well as we did."

"I didn't take it well. I avoided you for three days and drafted nine PR plans before I decided I couldn't make one until I told the father of my child I was having his baby!"

Zach's emerald eyes darkened when he tugged her closer, his grip tight but tender. She'd been battling fatigue, nausea and dizziness for weeks, but now it seemed the worst was behind her. The sexual tension that existed between them returned.

"You handling Eleanor Ferguson was quite possibly the sexiest moment I've ever witnessed."

Some of the fire went out of her. "Ever?"

His grin widened. "No. Not ever. Why don't I take you home and we can try for a new sexiest moment ever?"

"It's been a while."

"I know."

"You haven't complained." He'd been damn near angelic.

"I know."

She took a few steps closer in heels he hadn't bitched about tonight. Her shoes were a battle he'd allowed her to win. She fingered his collar and slipped her other hand down his buttoned shirt and over his black slacks.

A low grunt came from his throat when she pressed her lips to his, continuing her intimate massage down below. A few firm strokes and soon that part of him was much bigger than before.

He deepened their kiss, hands coming around to cup her ass. Every firm inch of him was flush against her and her hormones perked up.

"Zach." The breathy lilt of her voice was one she'd forgotten she'd possessed. "How about we take the car out in the yard and see if I can't break the sexiest moment record here."

"In the car?" His voice took on a husky quality and she laughed.

"Don't tell me you've never had a girl go down on you in a car."

"Not a girl as classy as you are," he all but growled.

"Good." She put a teasing kiss on the center of his mouth. "I love being first."

He wasn't wearing a tie, so she settled for dragging him to his car by the shirtsleeve. Zach followed, wide steps allowing for the part of him currently cheering the most for Pen's bold offer.

She liked that she had the power to affect him. It made her feel as if she could do anything. It made her feel like the woman she'd been before Cliff strangled her business into submission.

Zach put the car in gear and drove them behind the house and to the back of the grounds where trimmed trees and perfectly clipped grass met elegantly arranged flowers and shrubberies that were works of art.

"Your mom's going to freak about the landscaping when she sees the tire treads."

"First." Zach turned off the car and rolled the windows down. "That's the last time you mention my mom tonight. Second. I can't think of a second because my brains have relocated to my crotch."

"Hmm." Pen stifled her laughter to take advantage of the very sexy scene this created. Bucket leather seats, windows down, a warm Texas breeze heating the interior of the car and covering her neck in a light sheet of sweat where her hair fell. "I'm going to have to get a closer look to confirm."

Nothing felt better than turning him on. He wore lust so baldly—the flare of his nostrils, the widening of his pupils.

She undid his belt and released the clasp on his slacks. He was hard and ready, and when she slipped the waistband of his boxers past his erection, she licked her lips.

"You're doing that on purpose."

"Well. Yes." She rolled her eyes and he crushed another kiss onto her lips before she pulled away and lowered her head. She took him on her tongue, guiding his length deep into her mouth. His legs went rigid, knees locking as she continued working him over. His utterances were a mixture of swear words, reverent callouts to the Almighty, and incoherent groans. Just when she was starting to enjoy herself, he tugged her up and pressed another kiss onto her lips.

"Don't you dare move."

He jerked his pants over his hips and came around to her side of the car, pulling the door open and offering his hand like a prince helping her from a carriage. Except his pants were sagging open, his erection outlined by the tails of his untucked, wrinkled white shirt.

"No laughing," he warned.

She didn't laugh, and when the heels of her shoes sank into the soft earth, she kicked them off. Zach maneuvered them to a particularly soft patch of grass surrounded by bushes.

He hoisted her dress over her head, tossed her bra

aside and gently lowered her to the ground. He kissed her nipples, leaving them to pucker in the breeze while he unbuttoned his shirt and whipped it off his shoulders. Pants around his thighs, he didn't bother taking them off, and she couldn't think of a single reason he should.

She peeled her thong down her legs, ready for him and grateful to avoid another delay.

He slipped inside her, dropping his forehead to hers and letting out what might be a shudder. She tilted her hips and closed her eyes, head tossed back to appreciate the way she felt whenever he was inside her.

Full.

No.

Whole.

Her eyes flew open to meet his and he started moving again. Slowly, fluidly. Pumping in and out at a rhythm he set and she easily matched. Never had sex felt this intimate before Zach—before now. She reminded herself that her rounding belly and raging hormones were responsible for a plethora of emotions she hadn't experienced before.

Until he said, "You've never been more beautiful than you are now."

She pressed her fingertips to his mouth and he gave them a playful nip.

"You're saying that," she breathed as she braced for another sensual slide, "because you have to."

"I'm saying that—" another harsh breath from him blew her hair from her forehead "—because it's the truth."

She pushed on his chest. "On your back, cowboy."

His pause was momentary, but a second later he cupped her head and hip and, keeping them joined, shifted so that he was on his back instead.

"Impressive move with your pants around your knees." She smiled down at him.

"Thank ya, ma'am."

She rolled her eyes as he tipped a pretend cowboy hat, but his good humor erased when she pushed his chest to leverage herself up, and sank down on him again.

A hiss of air came from between his teeth, but he didn't close his eyes. No, he kept them right on her as she moved. His hands covered her breasts, his hips rising to meet hers.

And when her orgasm all but shattered her, Zach caught her against him, holding her hair from her face as he kissed her. He tilted his hips while she held on to the moving earth and then he came inside her.

The only sounds in the garden were crickets humming, the distant bark of a dog and Zach's father's shout on the air.

"Seriously?" The Zen of Penelope's orgasm washed away as her eyes went wide, her hands covering her breasts.

He let out a laugh. She speared him with a murderous glare before looking over her shoulder. He'd driven them deep into the gardens at the side of the house, so all his old man had seen—or could currently see—was the black blob of Zach's car.

And he and Pen were safely hidden on one side of it.

He sat up, keeping their connection as a tremor ran down his spine. Damn, he could have used a few more minutes to Zen out with her. Cradling her face, he gave her a swift kiss. Unfortunately, timing was of the essence before Rider called the cops.

"Get dressed," Zach told Pen. "I'll handle this."

Not since he was sixteen had he been caught with his pants around his ankles, and he wasn't starting today. He yanked them up, buckling his belt and pushing a hand through his hair.

He snatched his shirt off the ground and turned to find Pen, grass in her hair, roll her tiny scrap of a pair of panties up those long, golden legs.

He lifted her dress off the ground and handed it to her, noticing the grass stain a microsecond before she did. She merely shook her head and pulled it on, tugging it down and wadding the bra in her hand while Zach stepped into his shoes.

He spared one last glance the second his dad turned on the floodlight, enough to see her grow a little more irked, and in the process, a whole lot more beautiful.

Who knew that could happen?

"Zach?" his dad bellowed.

"It's me!" he called back. "Don't shoot!" He was only half kidding. From what he could see, Rider wasn't carrying a shotgun, but one could never be too careful.

So much for his parents never using this part of the house. He'd been sure this side was left to the staff or only opened up for parties.

His father strolled into the yard. Zach approached while he finished buttoning his white collared shirt.

"What in Sam hell are you doing?" Rider asked, his voice filled with mirth. "Trying to give me another heart attack? Because if your mother knew you were out here having sex in the petunias, she'd make sure I had one."

Rider turned to look over his shoulder but only briefly. They both knew Eleanor was in her bath by now with the TV on and a magazine in hand.

"I don't think those were petunias," Zach said in response.

"You two have your own place and you're carrying on like teenagers." His father sent a look over to the car where Pen sat in the front seat, elbow on the window, one hand hiding her face. "She knows I know that's her, right?"

"Yeah. She does." His own gaze lingered there a moment before he bid his dad adieu. "I'll pay to repair the lawn."

"You know I don't give a shit about that." Rider chuckled. "Get your girl home. Continue what you started indoors."

Zach's back straightened on his walk to the car, his swagger taking over. He was proud that this woman was with him. And that she'd offered to do dastardly things outside with him. Pen embodied the motto "work hard, play hard." He liked that a hell of a lot.

Zach reached the car and Rider called out, "'Night, Penny!" His loud boom of a guffaw heard as clear as day.

When Zach sank into his leather seat, Pen watched him for a solid thirty seconds. Fine by him. It gave him a moment to rebutton his shirt since he'd done it wrong on the walk over to his dad. He adjusted his seat belt and started the car, aware of her watching him the entire time.

"What?"

"Now your mom definitely hates me."

"She has no idea. Dad won't tell her." He reversed the car and drove through the grass.

Pen went stone silent.

Zach grasped her chin and turned her to face him, his car idling at the gate of his parents' gargantuan home. "I would never let her hate you. Give her time."

Pen's blue eyes softened with worry.

"I mean it. Give her a little time and she'll love you as much as my dad does."

He pulled out of the driveway and onto the street, the words he'd said wending around his brain. He'd meant them. Everyone loved Penelope—her clients, his siblings, his dad.

Do you? came the unplanned thought.

But that kind of love was different—he'd learned long ago that loving with his full heart wasn't rewarded. He wouldn't make that mistake again.

He drove home, arm leaning on his open window and the summer air blowing his hair.

Some thoughts were best left unexplored.

Fifteen

"Have your assistant return everything but this." Pen held up a tiny pair of shoes. "I can't part with these even though they're hysterically overpriced. The rest of it I can shop for online." She stood over the boutique baby clothes spread on Zach's king-size bed, her hands on her hips. There was a line in the center of her brows communicating her worry.

"Why?" He slid out of his suit jacket and hung it in his closet.

"Because a growing baby doesn't need extravagant—" she gestured to the stacks of gender-neutral clothing "—everything."

She'd set up the visit to the baby boutique for Saturday afternoon, and then they did something he'd never pictured himself doing. They shopped for their future son or daughter.

He'd purchased the clothing, shoes and toys that he and Pen carried out in the boutique's signature shiny bags, but he didn't stop there. He'd also snapped several pictures of furniture with his iPhone and sent them to his interior designer. Like right now, Pen had loved it but protested the inflated price tag.

"No one *needs* extravagant everything," Zach commented, unbuttoning his shirt. Pen paused, a yellow stuffed elephant rattle in her hand, and watched. He liked the way she looked at him—like he was her next meal. "Come take your clothes off."

"There's an invitation," she said with a laugh.

She tossed the elephant aside and came to him in the closet. Her eyes were sleepy despite it being hours before bedtime. After a shopping excursion and a late lunch, she looked beat. Not that it hindered her beauty at all.

Holding herself steady on the closet's interior wall, she slipped off one high-heeled shoe and then the other.

"Ah, so much better."

He'd lectured her nonstop about the damn shoes. It hadn't done any good.

"Just so we're clear," he said, shrugging off his shirt and tossing it into a hamper, "our child is entitled to have as many extravagant things as we see fit."

Her eyes roamed over his bare chest and he sucked in a breath to expand it farther. She smiled and gave him a playful shove.

"That's what I'd like to avoid. An *entitled* child." She

turned and lifted her hair and he pulled down the delicate zipper holding her dress closed. "I want our son or daughter to be loved and know that 'stuff' doesn't matter."

Zach ran his fingers down her exposed back, pausing at her bra strap. "This, too?"

She eyed him over her shoulder, a spark of want in her eyes mingling with the fatigue. As tempting as it was to seduce her, he'd digress.

"I'm going to work at home for a bit. Why not grab a nap?"

She slipped out of her dress, revealing smooth skin and a softly rounding belly. His chest flooded with possessiveness.

She covered her stomach and her brows bent.

He moved her hand and gave her a smile. "I like watching the changes in your body."

She cocked her head as if to challenge him. "You mean my growing girth?"

"You're making a human being. That takes up some real estate." It was a miracle in every sense of the word. "It's okay to take a break."

"I'll relax, but I want to keep my eye on the internet for our inevitable online debut."

The photographer had shown up like Pen arranged, snapping pictures of them inside the store through the windows as well as from across the street when they left the baby boutique.

"Right. The blogger."

"Not just any blogger." She hung her white dress and pulled on a pair of stretchy pale-pink pants.

He wanted to dispute the long white shirt covering her, until he realized he could see the shape of her nipples and the swell of her heavy breasts outlined by the thin fabric.

"The Dallas Duchess," Pen stated with a gesture that sent her breasts jiggling.

He pulled on a T-shirt and jeans and slipped into a pair of tennis shoes. "And she's important, I gather."

"Mmm-hmm. She keeps an eye on the Dallas movers and shakers. She'll have our photo up by this afternoon or tomorrow morning. I made sure of it."

That rogue twinkle in Pen's eye lit whenever she talked about her work. Whether she was digging a pair of canoodling actors out of a steaming pile of drama or arranging Zach's internet debut. He couldn't resist capturing some of that fire for himself. Not while she stood this close to him.

He wrapped an arm around her back and lowered his lips to hers, pressing her breasts to his chest as he made out with her long and slow. She tracked her fingers along his abs, and his belly clenched. He let out a low growl as she dropped from her toes and smiled up at him. He wanted her. Badly.

"You don't have to work right away, do you?" she asked with the quirk of one eyebrow.

"Hell, no," he answered, and then hoisted her in his arms and carried her the short distance to the bed.

She and Zach had played their roles while shopping earlier today. They'd kissed and hugged and smiled. She'd coached him this morning en route to the store, and he'd grumbled about the preparation, arguing that he wasn't that good of an actor.

Yet this afternoon, there he was, heat in his eyes and firmness in his kiss. But that wasn't all acting, now, was it? He'd been looking at her with heated eyes and owning her with his kisses since they'd re-met. And their going to bed together when they returned home was definitely par for course.

Mercy. She wondered how much of the sex she could blame on the hormones.

She finished packing the baby clothes and toys into the shopping bags for returning later. She was serious about not wanting an entitled child.

What she hadn't told him was that she'd also started thinking about the massive income gap between hers and Zach's annual earnings. Obviously, that'd always been a factor, but today especially, as she thought about providing for her son or daughter, she realized that half the child's time would be spent at Zach's house where everything would be provided in abundance. The other half? Spent with her where she'd earn a decent living, yes, and her child would never do without the necessities, but a two hundred dollar jumper wouldn't be hanging in the closet.

She shoved thoughts of the future aside and focused on the task in front of her. An email from the Dallas Duchess herself. The duchess confirmed that the blog would go live tomorrow.

So that was that.

Penelope and Zach would be making their announcement publicly soon after, confirming that yes, they were expecting. Being that Zach was both CEO of Ferguson

Oil and the mayor's brother, the story was news to any-one looking for gossip. The Fergusons weren't royal family status, but neither were they ignored. Their staggering good looks paired with their billionaire incomes made the two brothers and sister popular in this city.

"Way to pick a baby daddy," Pen joked aloud. But she didn't feel an ounce of regret for going to bed with Zach—or moving in with him. Like Cinderella, her fairy tale would soon come to an end.

She glanced around the living room—masculine browns and earth tones like his apartment with a touch of hominess in shades of blue—and admitted she liked nesting here, even if it wasn't permanent. There would be time to ready her apartment—to *acquire* an apartment. In the meantime, she would be treated like a queen.

She scraped her bottom lip with her teeth as she turned over the shallow thoughts. Pen wasn't accustomed to being dependent on anyone but herself. Her mother had raised her to be her own godmother, not the princess flailing about wearing only one glass slipper.

Once upon a time Pen had been involved with a client who had offered to "take care of everything" and look how that'd ended up. She'd vowed never to let her guard down again—yet here she was, breaking her rules for Zach.

Had she traded her pluck for comfort? Was she shallow? Or, was Zach different? Was what they had something she'd never truly experienced—the beginning of a trusting relationship that might lead to that elusive beast: love?

Surely not.

Pen had looked forward to the day she'd moved away from home. She'd excelled at running her own life. So well, in fact, she'd begun advising others how to run theirs and charging them for it.

Right now she was simply being practical. Her affinity for Zach—the doting as well as the sex—was temporary. Soon, she'd have a child to raise. A baby to nurse. And still have her business to run. She wouldn't have time for frivolous relationships any more than she'd have time for a mani-pedi on a Sunday afternoon.

They were sacrifices she was willing to make. And with Zach in the picture, it wasn't as if she'd be doing it alone. She'd have help. Albeit not living under this same roof, because that was impractical. But they'd have shared custody...

The sentence trailed to a muted end and her head spun.

Zach *would* share custody, wouldn't he? He wouldn't try and take her child from her? Of course he wouldn't. Unless...he dated someone else in the future. Maybe things would get serious and the woman would want to play a bigger role in their child's life.

Pen's eyebrows snapped together. She didn't want their child raised by another woman. And what if that other woman ended up like Yvonne, with no scruples and a money-grubbing attitude? Zach hadn't only dated Yvonne, he'd *married* her.

"Whoa. You okay?" Zach stepped into the living room, casual attire doing nothing to dash the air of power surrounding him. Power and money. "You look… not okay."

She could imagine. If her face revealed any of her thoughts about a future custody battle, she must resemble a gladiator readying for a fight. Pen launched into a conversation without any preempting whatsoever.

"I wanted to talk to you about custody of our baby." The words were as thick as wet sand, but she got them out.

He frowned as he came deeper into the living room and sat next to her on the couch. She set aside her phone.

"We'll share it. Obviously," she stated.

"When the time comes." His eyelids narrowed. "Your home is here, Pen. I'm in no hurry to have you gone."

"But eventually, I'll leave."

"Maybe. Maybe not."

"Zach." He'd been saying that a lot and she'd gone along, but what happened when her carriage turned into a pumpkin? "Eventually. I'll leave. I hope you won't fight me for full custody of our child."

"I'm not going to fight you for anything involving our child." He tipped his head toward the bags of clothing she'd set by the front door. "Except you keeping the purchases we made at the boutique."

"It's too much."

"Penelope." He placed his hand on her neck, his thumb sliding along her jaw as he met her eyes with his potent green stare. "I'm having a child, too. Buying for our baby, taking care of you, are the only ways I know how to participate. Let me."

His eyebrows lifted into an earnest expression and

she closed her eyes. Maybe she was too emotional about…well, everything. Shaking her head, she said, "I'm sorry. I'm worrying about everything."

"Worry about one thing. What you want for dinner. And then tell me and I'll either make it or have it delivered." He stood from the couch, bending and placing a kiss on her forehead. She watched him walk out of the room, his sure, strong steps and presence making every hectic thought in her tired brain calmer.

She might not be in love with the father of her baby, but she could admit that the biggest part she'd miss about the princess treatment was going to be Zach himself.

Sixteen

Zach had adapted to his role as CEO of Ferguson Oil easily, sliding into the slot left for him by his father like he was meant to be there all along. Kind of made him wonder if he'd been avoiding his destiny when he left for Chicago.

Which kind of made him wonder if no matter what direction he ran, he would've still ended up right back here in this very position: father-to-be of a baby boy or girl.

The night he took Penelope home from the jazz club, he'd never considered that they might someday share a child. Shortsighted? A bit. Sex equaled babies for lots of couples. But he'd been in the habit of chasing his physical desires rather than worrying about outcomes.

He rubbed eyes that were crossing to center. When he

reopened them, the spreadsheet on his computer screen blurred. He redirected his gaze to the wall clock to see it was past five; another day had gotten away from him.

His assistant patched through a call. "Mr. Ferguson, it's the mayor on line three."

"It's Zach, and my brother's name is Chase," he reminded Sam, who insisted on the formality.

"Yes, sir," Sam replied. "Will you be taking the mayor's call?"

Zach shook his head at the futility and answered the line.

"Chase," he said into the phone. "What's up?"

"Were you planning on telling me about my niece or nephew?" came his brother's terse question.

Zach's eyes sank closed as he pressed his fingers into his eyelids. "Shit, Chase. I meant to tell you."

What an oversight.

"You mean before my press conference where a reporter asked if *I* was expecting a baby because you and Penelope were spotted baby shopping over the weekend? Yeah. You should've told me."

There was a twist neither Zach nor Pen had seen coming.

"The press assumed it was you who was having a baby?"

"Me and the woman on my arm at the charity event at our parents' house. She's a financial adviser and I offered to show her around." Zach could tell by his brother's grumbling that he was serious about the woman being an acquaintance. The mayor wasn't into spur of the moment or temporary relationships. For Chase, every woman on his arm had a purpose, a reason for being there.

"That photo of us was supposed to pad our public announcement of the pregnancy, not start a rumor mill about you."

He grunted at the irony. Chase was the star of the Ferguson show no matter what happened to any of them.

"Stefanie already knew." Chase's tone was clipped.

"Not on purpose. I let it slip and swore her to secrecy."

"Mom and Dad. They know. *She* had to tell me." Before Zach could make an excuse about how it'd been a busy week, his brother added, "What the hell are you doing?"

Zach straightened his back, on alert. "What's that supposed to mean?"

"Your engagement with Penelope Brand is fake. Or *was* anyway. Has that changed?" His brother believed that relationships had beginnings and endings that were mapped out ahead of time. But Zach didn't have to think that way. He wasn't the one who'd put his balls in the public sling.

"Not that I have to explain anything to you," Zach told his brother, "but Pen was pregnant the night of your birthday party. We just didn't know it at the time."

Chase uttered a curse under his breath. "Are you planning on making it a real engagement to go along with your real future child?"

"What if I do?"

"Then I suggest you consider how long you want to keep this up."

Off his chair, Zach felt his blood pressure rise. "Come again?"

"You're not the only one involved, Zach. You'll have a child soon and you can't marry Pen because it sounds *fun*. The stakes are sky-high."

"I know that." Zach's words gritted from between his clenched teeth. "I can handle my own life. You're just worried how my actions will affect your precious career."

"Wrong. I'm reminding you because I've seen the two of you together. You're behaving like a couple. A *real* one. Has that sunk in for you yet?"

He thought it had. Until Chase pointed out he'd noticed a difference. Zach dated casually, sure, but he felt like his brother was referring to a relationship in Zach's past—way in his past. One in particular that hadn't ended well.

"I'm handling it," Zach repeated rather than broach the topic of Lonna.

"Let's start over." Chase blew out a heavy breath. "What I should've said, rather than dispense a big brother lecture, was that I'm excited for you. For our family. The first baby is a big deal."

"You're jealous you didn't get there first." Zach allowed a sideways smile when his brother chuckled.

"Yeah, you win."

But Chase's words settled in the center of Zach's chest. A baby *was* a big deal. So was an engagement. And Penelope living in his house.

"I'm taking this seriously." Zach felt the urge to clarify. After a pause, Chase spoke.

"How is she?"

"Healthy. Gorgeous. Stubborn." *Impossible*, he mentally added. "Returned every bit of the baby clothes we purchased because they were too expensive."

"You call that stubborn? I call it practical."

"Stubborn," Zach reiterated.

"Almost as stubborn as you." Chase wasn't wrong. "Way to pick 'em, brother. How about you?"

"How about me what?" He closed the spreadsheet and powered down the computer.

"How are you?"

"I'm good. I'm fine."

Chase waited, not buying the blow-off.

Zach sat back down and rested his forehead on his hand. Then he confessed something to Chase he hadn't told anyone. "I'm trying not to screw everything up for my child."

"You'll figure it out. You're not a screw-up, Zach. You try everything once, and that's not a bad thing. I'm the careful planner, and knowing what I know of Penelope, I'm guessing she's a careful planner, too."

"The *carefulest*."

"You'll find your way. You don't know how to fail. You stay on the balls of your feet and roll with the punches better than anyone I've ever known."

The vote of confidence from the man he admired most, second to Dad, meant the world to Zach. His throat thick with emotion, he couldn't even manage a muttered "Thanks." Zach wasn't the get-choked-up kind, but *damn*.

"When do you find out if I'm having a niece or a nephew?"

He smiled at his brother's use of the monikers again—if he wasn't mistaken, Chase was looking forward to being an uncle.

"Next week." Zach swept his eyes to his desk calendar to confirm.

"Tell me *first* this time."

"We'll see. Stefanie has already mentioned some gender reveal something-or-another."

Chase's reaction was a mumbled curse followed by, "Of course she did."

Zach ended the call with his brother as a quick knock came from Sam who ushered in Mara, his bubbly and completely kick-ass CFO.

"Zach." Her eyes sparkled with interest. Not in him personally—he'd never before met someone so happily married—but like she knew something he didn't. "Here are the reports you asked for."

She handed them over and then stood smiling at him. He studied her with a frown for a moment, then decided to give it up. She knew. It was evident in every jittering line of her body.

"We can't officially announce it yet, so I appreciate your discretion."

Mara clapped her hands and let out a discreet "Yay!" To his shock, she rounded the desk and gave him a quick side hug.

"I'm so thrilled for you both! When Vic and I had our baby it was exciting and scary and amazing. You're going to do great. And Penelope is so gorgeous—you'll have the prettiest baby in the world! Second to mine, of course."

Okay, that made him smile.

Mara skipped away. As she pulled the door shut, she gave him a wink in the diminishing gap and said in a stage whisper, "I won't breathe a word to anyone."

"Thanks, Mara."

She shut the door behind her and he glanced at his desk calendar where he'd jotted Pen's ultrasound with the shorthand *ult* in case of wandering eyes.

Chase was right. Zach would slide seamlessly into the role of father as well as he'd slid into CEO at Ferguson Oil. And if he had a hiccup or two along the way, Pen would be there to bail him out—planner that she was.

Smile on his face, he relaxed in his chair.

They had this.

A blur of elegance from outside the wall of her glass office windows caught Penelope's eye. She blinked once, then twice to make sure what she was seeing wasn't a mirage.

Nope.

It was Zach's mother, all right.

Pen beckoned her in and rounded her desk. "Elle. This is a surprise."

Especially since she didn't know how Elle knew where she worked. Pen's mind went to their last interaction. Elle reacted poorly to the news of the pregnancy and then Pen and Zach had sex in the woman's flower beds.

Real classy, Pen.

Elle clutched a large camel-colored handbag and gestured to the white leather couch. "May I sit?"

"Yes, please. I was just wrapping up." Pen sat with her, pretty sure the fluttering in her stomach wasn't her baby but nerves instead. Maybe a bit of both.

"How are you feeling?"

"Lately, much better than before."

"I'm so glad for you! When I was pregnant with Stefanie, I remember the worst morning sickness and bloating." Elle waved a hand dismissively. "If I had that with Chase and Zach, I've blocked it because all I remember is how painful the birth was." Elle let out a soft laugh and then a look of chagrin colored her features. "I didn't mean to alarm you. What a thing to say."

"It's fine, really." Pen meant it. "Believe it or not, I've heard a thing or two about childbirth being painful."

A gap in the conversation settled in the room like a third party. Pen filtered through her brain for a topic to fill the dead air. Luckily, Elle filled it for her.

"I came by to apologize for my poor reaction when you came to tell us about your bundle of joy."

"Thank you. We sprung it on you, so it's understandable."

"No. It's not. Rider's mother wanted to throttle us when she found out I was pregnant with Chase before the wedding." Elle rolled her eyes, and it wasn't hard to imagine what she'd looked like as a much younger woman railing against her future in-laws. "I've made a few mistakes with my children when it comes to their relationships. Being a matriarch is a tough business."

Pen's eyebrows climbed her forehead.

"Oh, you think the men are in charge in our family?" Elle picked at an invisible piece of lint on her skirt and smoothed her hand over the material. "We let them think that. You're a strong woman. You're an amazing addition to this family."

Guiltily, Pen looked at her lap. She felt like she was lying by letting Elle believe Pen and Zach were really together, but there was no way to unravel the lie without causing damage to everyone.

"I'm about to overstep my boundaries," Elle said next.

Pen lifted her head to meet eyes with the older woman.

"Do you know about Lonna?"

The name didn't bring forth the barest whisper of familiarity. "I don't think so."

"I don't know that Zach knows *I* know how in-deep he was with her. But I'm his mother. I knew."

Pen was dancing in dangerous territory. Part of her wanted to ask Elle about the woman from Zach's past, and another part of her felt loyalty to her fake fiancé. In the end, her curiosity won.

"Who was she?"

"They dated when Zach was in his midtwenties. She was a few years older than him and there was always something I didn't like about her. Her strength wasn't so much strength as fierce independence. Independence she cherished over our son's heart.

"Zach would sooner die than admit to us that she broke his heart, but I could tell. He was different after her. After they split, he withdrew. Then he moved to Chicago and we swore we'd never see him again."

That was why he moved to Chicago? *Away* from a woman? Rather than chasing a dream? Did that make a difference?

Yes, Pen realized.

She'd run from Chicago because of a business endeavor—because she'd needed to reform her reputation. Not because she couldn't bear to be in the same state as an ex.

"My point of telling you this isn't to worry you, Penelope." Elle placed her hand gently over Pen's, making Pen wonder if the worry showed on her brow. "My point is to let you know that I'd started believing he'd never commit to another woman. Not seriously." Elle sneered, but still managed to look elegant doing it. "We all know that Yvonne debacle was a blip of rash stupidity."

"Let's hope," Pen blurted.

"I know my son. I'm right. But here you are, and Penelope, believe me when I tell you that Zach has finally given his heart to someone. To you. He wouldn't get engaged again so soon unless he meant it."

Pen's smile was as brittle as burned paper. *Or unless he wanted to get out of hot water with his raving lunatic of an ex-wife.*

"You're going to be an amazing mother, Penelope, and you'll have a dedicated husband and father at your side. Trust me when I tell you that."

Pen blinked her eyes against forming tears and when her vision cleared, Elle was reaching into her handbag and bringing out a blue-and-white crocheted blanket.

"This was Zach's when he was a baby. His great-grandmother Edna made it for him." She handed over the soft pile of yarn, a few frayed ends tied into knots. "He'll kill me if I tell you this, but what the hell." Elle cupped her mouth with one hand and stage-whispered, "He slept with it until he was eleven."

Pen laughed and lost the battle with a few tears that streaked down her cheeks. She swiped at them quickly, and then held the blanket in both hands.

Her baby would someday be a grown man or woman and have a history—a history with two parents who pretended to be in love. A history that had to be history.

The more distance she put between this baby's birth and her living with and pretending with Zach, the better. She wasn't being fair to anyone. Not Zach's siblings or parents, or her own parents, or especially her child.

Lying was going to have a ripple effect on her baby's life and she couldn't allow that. As kind as it was for Elle to stop by and apologize and declare her son's love for Pen, there was one fact that remained unchallenged.

Zach and Pen, while they liked each other just fine, weren't in love. They didn't share their plans for a long future, or discuss grandmothers or past heartbreaks.

They shared plans and a schedule. They shared a bed.

And those things did not a love story make.

Seventeen

Pen blew out a breath, lying on a table in the doctor's office and not feeling the least little bit relaxed. Today she and Zach would learn if they were having a son or a daughter and the anticipation was almost too much to handle.

She hadn't told Zach that his mother had stopped by to chat. Reason being, she wasn't sure how to broach the topic. The Lonna Story was his story to tell, and frankly, that he hadn't told her was…well, *telling*. Pen and Zach were in deep together. They were engaged—kinda—expecting a baby and he'd pretty much decreed that she wasn't moving out.

Yet when it came to divulging his personal past, he was silent. Which could only mean one thing. Zach had been hurt and quite possibly wasn't over the mysterious Lonna.

"How are you doing, Ms. Brand?" The doctor stepped into the room. Dr. Cho was young and beautiful, her silken black hair tied back at the base of her neck. Her kind, almond-shaped eyes swept to Zach and she nodded in greeting.

Zach promised Pen that Dr. Cho was the best in Dallas. He'd insisted on the very best care and Pen hadn't argued. She might not relish the idea of piles of outrageous baby clothing, but she agreed that the best care for their child was the *only* care.

"I'm nervous," Pen admitted.

"Nothing to be nervous about." Dr. Cho squirted clear goo onto a flat plastic ultrasound paddle and warned it'd be cold. "How about you, Dad?"

Pen's eyes clashed with Zach's and he held her gaze while he said, "Doing just fine."

"Good."

Cold, definitely, but the shock of the chill faded as Pen searched the image on screen for her baby. And there it was. A whooshing sound of the heartbeat and what actually resembled a human being.

Incredible.

Tears pricked the corners of her eyes but accompanied a resilient smile. Zach breathed a "Wow" next to her, his gaze glued to the screen, his mouth ajar.

It was a miracle.

An unexpected, unrelenting miracle.

After a few minutes and measurements, Dr. Cho asked if they'd like to know the sex.

"Yes," Pen and Zach answered eagerly—both on the same page. This little gem had given them enough surprises.

Pen held her breath and wondered if Zach did the same. Then Dr. Cho told them the sex of their baby.

"It's incredible, isn't it?" Zach said on the ride home from the doctor's office. Hearing the heartbeat had been one thing, but seeing their child on the screen and knowing a little Ferguson would soon be entering their lives was unbelievable.

Pen was lying back against the headrest, the A/C cranked up so high her hair blew in the air coming from the vent. August in Texas was hell. But Zach didn't mind the heat or the fact that he had to lift his voice to talk over the vent forcing out cool air. He was on cloud nine.

In spite of today's announcement ruining a particular surprise.

He pulled into the garage of his new house and rounded the car to open Pen's door for her. She wore a long white dress and heels, but her shoes were lower heeled than her normal nine-to-five wear. His favorite part of the dress was the wispy material that slitted up both sides showing peeks of her smooth calves when she walked as well as the off-the-shoulder straps that showcased not only a gorgeous collarbone but also cleavage that was going for the World's Record for holding Zach's undivided attention.

Inside he gave her the bad news. "I had a surprise planned, and now it's not as good of a surprise unless you want to leave the house for a day or two so I can fix it."

She slanted her head and narrowed one eye, her smile playful. "What'd you do?"

He shook his head in chagrin, but found his smile wasn't going anywhere, either. "You're gonna laugh."

"Now I have to know."

Here went nothing. Time to own it.

He led her through the house and upstairs to the baby's room. His designer had come in and furnished the room with a crib and dresser and changing table— the same furniture that Pen had pointed out at Love & Tumble. The style was what he preferred: clean, simple, warm. No pastels or frilly anything. His designer had insisted on beige with white crown molding running along the center of the wall, which he at first protested. She'd argued it was "the perfect blank palette ready for a splash of color" for when they found out the sex. When he'd first showed Pen, she loved it. Zach turned the knob, gave Pen one last lift of his eyebrows and pushed the door wide.

He was right about the laughing.

His surprise? Decking their child's room floor to ceiling in Dallas Cowboys paraphernalia.

"You were awfully certain we were having a boy," Pen said with a giggle as she stepped into the room.

"I was." And then the ultrasound proved him wrong. He shook his head but he didn't have a single ounce of regret about the outcome.

A daughter with Pen's gorgeous blue eyes? He'd take it. He'd have to scare off testosterone-infused boys once she was a teen, but he'd worry about that later. This was Texas. He had a shotgun.

"Zach." Pen searched the room, her eyes landing on framed posters of the players, a mobile featuring footballs and cowboy hats, and on the shelf, a signed football in a case. He'd gone all out. The mother of his child faced him.

Fingers shoved in his front pockets, he explained with a shrug. "Maybe she's a Cowboys fan."

"Clearly you're one."

"Honey, I'm in Dallas. I'm a Cowboys fan." He took a look around for himself. He was pretty damn proud of the cool stuff he'd picked out. "We can tone it down a little."

"A little?" She lifted a blanket thrown over the crib that resembled a football field—green with the yard-age marked in white. "Really?"

"I wanted to surprise you. You're surprised. Mission accomplished."

"Yeah. I'm surprised, all right." She rested her hand on the crib and palmed her belly, not yet as big as it would be. He felt a firm tug in his chest. "I'm grateful that it's a girl after your mother told me how big you two boys were."

"When did she tell you that?" She hadn't mentioned talking with his mother.

"Last week. She stopped by my office."

A pair of chairs flanked a side table with a lamp and, yes, a Cowboys lampshade, and Pen sat in one and beckoned for him to sit in the other one.

She opened the side table drawer as he sat, coming

out with his crocheted baby blanket he hadn't seen in decades.

"She dropped this off for our daughter."

"It's blue." He took it, then gestured around the room. "Matches the theme."

"She apologized for her reaction. I know she wanted to smooth things over. She wasn't proud of herself. I didn't hold it against her, though."

"No, you wouldn't," he said. "You take issues on. You don't push them off on others." And just so Pen didn't think he meant it any other way, he amended, "That's a compliment."

"I know it is." She inhaled and held her breath for a few seconds and that tug in his chest turned uncomfortable. What else did his mother say when she stopped by?

"Is there more?"

Pen released the breath she'd been holding. "Elle said… Well, she brought up a woman named Lonna. Then she told me she never thought you'd fall in love again."

His shoulders stiffened. He kneaded the super-soft blanket in his hands, avoiding looking at Pen. His mother knew about Lonna, of course, but what gave her the right to barge in on his fiancée and offer her opinion on his heart, for God's sake?

"I bring it up because your mom thinks we're in love."

That lifted his head. He watched her carefully. "She doesn't know anything about Lonna." The edge in his voice forced him from his seated position. He dropped the baby blanket on the chair and paced to the door.

"Did you love her? For real?"

Anger stopped him in his tracks. As if he was only capable of "unreal" relationships? His eyes went to the stairs leading to the front door, but he didn't run away from problems any longer. He ran toward them. He ran back to Texas, ran headfirst into a Vegas wedding to prove to himself he was "fine" and ran straight to Pen when she delivered news most men would've run *from*.

He faced Pen, leaned on the jamb and shoved his fingers back into his pockets. She lifted her hand to push a lock of hair from her face, and the diamond ring he'd slipped onto her finger glinted in the sunlight streaming in through the Cowboys-blue curtains.

Zach was a lot of things but he wasn't a liar. So, he told Pen the truth. "Yes."

She took the news well, simply nodding. But she wasn't done.

"Did you go to Chicago because she broke up with you?"

In part, but he saw no reason to explain himself. "Yes."

Pen took that news well, too, but had one final question for him. "Are you over her?"

That question required no hesitation. "Yes."

If he wasn't mistaken, that was a relieved breath Pen just blew out. "Your mother believes we're in love, Zach. She thinks this is our happily-ever-after and I couldn't correct her."

"You and my mother had quite the conversation."

"I didn't know she was going to go into all of that.

And I honestly wouldn't ask you to clarify any of this if it wasn't for what lies before us."

That statement settled into the room like an elephant.

"Which is what?" She kept making decisions and telling him last. He didn't like it.

"When we announce the sex of the baby at our surprise shower, we should also announce that we won't be getting married. Hear me out." She held a hand in front of her as if to silence him, probably because he'd filled his chest full of air to protest how they didn't have to do anything. Before she said more, he managed to blow out one question in an infuriated tone.

"What surprise shower?"

"I'm guessing that's why your sister asked me to clear a spot on my calendar in two weeks for a 'cake-tasting appointment.'" Pen used air quotes. "It sounded very…suspicious. Plus, she asked that we tell no one the sex of the baby—not even her."

"The gender reveal," he mumbled. "She'd mentioned she wanted to host one and then never said another word." He'd hoped she would forget about it. He should've known better.

Zach swiped a hand over his forehead, frustrated. Why the hell was everyone arranging parties around him, talking about him like he was a backdrop? Like he was a store mannequin. He was the one who arranged his life. It was *his* life, dammit.

"Before you blow up, let me finish."

He gave her the most patient glare he could manage, aware of the heat warming his face.

"We thank everyone for the gifts. And we hold

hands—I'll take this off first—" she waggled her ring finger "—and then we'll let everyone know that while we'll be living separate lives we are very much going to raise our daughter together. Everyone will be so overjoyed to learn that we're having a girl that I'm betting they won't even focus on the fact that we're announcing a breakup."

"We're not breaking up."

"Zach." She stood, her hand protectively over her middle. "We're not in love. You can't believe our sex-soaked relationship isn't going to fall apart. There's nothing holding us together except our attraction for each other. What about when that fades?"

"What if it doesn't?" He saw no reason to put a head-stone on what they had. Not yet. They had time.

"Come on. We've both been in relationships. Did the infatuation stage last forever?"

He ground his back teeth together. "We're not break-ing up. Wear the ring on Sunday. We're not doing this."

"You can't run from this forever."

"I'm not running from anything." To illustrate his point, he stepped deeper into the room and stood in front of her. "I'm here, right in front of you. And that's where I'm staying until I decide. Not you. Not my mother. Not my family. Not the duchess of fucking Dallas. *Me*."

Eighteen

Pen smoothed cocoa butter over her stomach, determined to avoid stretch marks at any cost. She'd read that moisturizing helped, and she'd started her nightly routine almost right after she found out she was pregnant.

As she ran her hand over her rounding belly, she considered the warring feelings inside her.

Frustration with Zach. Frustration with herself. Amusement for how he'd decorated the room for a son. Admiration at the way he was determined to be a good father. And the biggest: so much love for her unborn baby, she was ready to burst with it.

If she was being honest with herself, that love was inching closer and closer to Zach himself. Encircling him and swallowing him up in it. But she couldn't confuse her love for their daughter for romantic love with him. They weren't the same.

When she'd asked him about Lonna, he'd confirmed one of Pen's biggest fears. Falling in love meant you could lose it all. And for all of Zachary Ferguson's bliss-chasing, he'd drawn a very distinct boundary around true love.

Romantic love had no place in his plans. Not any longer. Not since Lonna.

It was unfair.

Unfair because for the first time in her life, Pen feared she was starting to fall in love…with a man incapable of loving her back.

"Hey," came a soft rumble from the doorway.

Pen spun the lid on the lotion and set it on her night-stand. "Hey."

Zach's hooded eyes and sideways smile had replaced his flattened mouth and ruddy complexion. After their conversation in the baby's room, he'd mumbled something about working and shut himself in his office. She hadn't seen him since.

They weren't fighting. Not really. They just had very different views of the way things were.

For Penelope, she needed to leave before she fell for him and couldn't pull away as easily. For Zach, there was no hurry because falling for her wasn't a remote possibility.

Perhaps acknowledging that was what hurt most.

"I overreacted," he said, walking into the room. "Did you eat?"

"All I do is eat." She gave him a tired smile. "Did you?"

"Just ate a sandwich."

"Dinner at nine-thirty."

"Bachelor," he explained.

Her heart squeezed at the word. That was the problem. Even with his pregnant fiancée in the house, Zach still considered himself single.

His eyes searched the room before landing on her again. "I don't want you to move out. I don't want to miss anything."

She had to close herself off from the sincerity in his voice. There was a bigger picture—the baby girl residing in her growing belly.

"You won't miss anything," she promised. "My stomach is going to get larger, my ankles more swollen, my temper more out of control. It might even get as bad as yours."

He shook his head in agreement. "I'm sorry about that."

He sat on the bed and lifted the delicate edge of her short cotton nightie, skimming the lace hemline up to expose her thighs. When one large, warm hand landed on her skin, she found it suddenly hard to breathe.

This was such a bad idea. Sealing her tumultuous feelings with sex wouldn't bring her closer to a resolution but take her further from it.

"How tired are you?" His green eyes sought hers.

Who was she fooling? Could she really convince herself she wasn't in love with him? Not when he looked at her the way he looked at her now. Not when he was watching the monitor at Dr. Cho's office with rapt attention and pride. And not when he touched her—especially when he touched her.

Zach claimed her as his that night in the mayor's mansion. She thought then it'd been about sex and physical love, but now she realized that claim was staked deep in her heart and soul. And the proof of it was incubating in her womb.

"Not too tired," she whispered, her eyes glazing over with staunch acceptance. She'd rather have him than not—even if it drove another stake into her lovesick heart.

He leaned forward to place a kiss on her bared shoulder. His tongue flicked under the strap, then dragged up her neck, giving her all of his attention like no other woman in his past or present who'd commanded it.

Warmth flooded her tummy, the flutter between her legs having everything to do with a million jettisoning hormones. She buried her lovelorn emotions into a deep, dark corner of her being and focused on the present. Focused on giving in to her physical needs—and riding Zach like the cowboy she once thought he was.

Her nightie was gone in a whisper as he lifted it over her head and tossed it to the floor. He smoothed his hand along her swollen belly, moving to her breasts next.

Lying back, she closed her eyes as his amazing mouth skated over one nipple then the other. The sensations assaulting her brought an end to the warring emotions in her chest and the thoughts littering her brain. And when his hands moved between her thighs and stroked, every ounce of her attention went there. Nothing felt as natural, as all-consuming, as making love with Zachary Ferguson.

His lips were at home on her body—*anywhere* on her body. Every inch of her belonged to him.

She reached for his T-shirt, tugging at it weakly. "Off."

"Yes, ma'am." There was the drawl she loved so much. He whipped off his shirt to reveal his chest and once again, breathing became difficult. Was it any wonder she let herself indulge in what she thought would only be one night with him? Was it any wonder she indulged now?

She took a page from Zach's book and released her worries of responsibility and the future, letting go like dandelion fluff on a thick summer's breeze. She focused on his physicality instead.

His broad shoulders, round like he spent the day hauling hay bales instead of sliding a mouse across his desk. His biceps, straining as he shoved his jeans to his knees. Thick thighs, covered in coarse, dark-blond hair and leading down to sturdy feet. All of him was gorgeous. And for the moment, hers.

"You keep looking at me like that, Penelope Brand, and I'm not going to last a minute." His green eyes sparked in challenge. His dimple dented his cheek as he shucked his boxers.

She embraced the idea of behaving like an out-of-control teenager. Pen had always been drawn to stability…until she'd moved to Dallas. Until she'd laid eyes on Zach. He made her embrace the moment. Made her live in right now.

His hot skin came in contact with hers and she could've sworn she felt sparks dance on her skin. He stripped her panties down her legs and once she was naked, pressed every part of himself against her.

She moaned. He was perfect.

He was hers. In a superficial, temporary sense, but nonetheless *hers*.

"Remember to pretend to be surprised," Penelope told Zach as they stepped up to the entryway of the hotel. At the top floor stood the Regal Room, their destination. A popular choice for parties of the upscale variety. She'd never been, but knew about it, and had recommended it for some of her more elite clients in Dallas.

"Should I add clutching my heart for effect?" Zach leaned over to ask, his voice low. Then pressed the button for the elevator.

"That might be poor form since Rider will be there."

"Oh, right." But his smirk hinted that he'd already figured that out.

This was the way things had been in the two weeks since their argument that ended in bed. They'd ended up in bed several times since and each interaction was like the last. Penelope fell deeper in love with him, and Zach maintained his position as kind, caring father of her child.

It should be enough. She wanted to be the woman for whom it would be enough. Where his loyalty and limited offerings would be substantial for as long as they lasted.

But they weren't.

It was the wrong time to broach the topic, but she'd been unable to summon the bravery to do it before. Now or never, as the saying went. So while the elevator zipped them to their destination, she blurted, "I'm going to announce that the wedding is on hold when I announce that we're having a daughter."

His steely glare matched the hardness of his jaw. "Penelope."

"I'm not asking permission." She lifted her chin. It was past time she pulled the plug on the relationship that was rapidly eating away at her heart.

"This isn't—" he started, but the elevator doors swished open at that moment.

They stepped out of the elevator and were greeted by a sea of smiling faces, very few of which she recognized.

Collectively, a shout rose in the room. "Congratulations!"

The "surprise" baby shower wasn't pink and blue or even green and yellow. The palette was a sophisticated blend of white and gold, right down to the confetti now littering the floor. Balloons tied with gold-and-black ribbon were suspended from the main table, which boasted flutes of champagne and an array of tapas displayed on elegant platters.

The banner draping the back of the room was white with gold metallic cursive lettering reading, "It's a baby!"

A few flashes from cameras snapped as Stefanie broke off from the crowd and enveloped Pen into a warm hug. Pen held on a beat longer than she expected. Ending the engagement with Zach also would mean distancing herself from his family, and she was going to miss Stef when she left.

"We're very surprised," Pen said, including Zach, who stood at her side like a wall. She quirked an eyebrow at him and his mouth pulled into a tight smile for the benefit of their guests. Yes, probably her timing wasn't the best on telling him her plans.

Stef hugged her brother next. "I know you hate surprises, Zach, but try to lighten up."

"I'll try," came his gruff response.

"So, I lied about this being a cake-tasting," Stefanie said, gesturing to a round table off to the side, "but we do have cake."

Chase, Elle and Rider emerged from the crowd next to deliver hugs and welcomes. Elle, in particular, was notably excited.

"Granddaughter or grandson?" she asked Pen conspiratorially. "One blink for a girl, two for a boy."

"No! Absolutely not." Stefanie positioned herself between her mother and Penelope. "Nine o'clock is the announcement, and not a moment before."

"Nine o'clock," Pen said, her own smile faltering. A quick glance to Zach confirmed that his was gone completely. "Uh, Stefanie, this room is amazing. The party, the food. Everything looks incredible."

She had to focus on her appreciation for what Stef had done, and pray that she could somehow dismantle the engagement and announce that she was expecting a girl without ruining the vibe of the party, or undoing Stef's hard work. She hoped Stef would understand and forgive her.

Stefanie put a hand on her hip and gestured like a model on *The Price is Right*. "I did it myself. I mean, yeah, okay, I had a team helping, but the ideas came out of my brain."

"Well, it's incredible," Pen said, meaning it. "If I need a party of any kind in the future, I'm coming to you."

"Sparkling grape juice." Stef plucked a flute from a waiter's tray. "I put little purple ribbons on the non-alcoholic drinks for you." Pen accepted her bubbly drink, a lump settling in her throat. She forced it down and called up her party smile again.

"Come see what else I have planned." Stef wrapped her arm around Pen's and led her away. Pen gladly took the reprieve—anything to keep Zach from bringing up the conversation she'd railroaded him with in the elevator.

He was easy to avoid over the next two hours given that Stef had filled the evening with games—albeit sophisticated ones.

"We're adults," Stef had said with committed seriousness. "I'm not melting chocolate bars in diapers, or asking guests to guess your belly width with lengths of toilet paper."

"Thank you for that." As sisters went, Zach hit the jackpot. Pen ignored the feeling of melancholy that swept over her. No matter where Pen and Zach ended up, Stef would always be their daughter's aunt. Pen would hold on to that.

Dessert was a selection of miniature cakes or cupcakes, and cake pops on sticks, all decorated in white fondant with edible gold sprinkles. Pen sampled the sweets, and drank down another sparkling grape juice as she played coy about her baby's sex. She'd lost count of how many times she'd told someone "Sorry. The announcement is at nine."

About twenty minutes before the evening's most anticipated hour, she found an opening and slipped away from the crowd. Zach and Chase were speaking to their grandparents' friends and since Pen had already spoken with Rudy and Ana, she knew their conversation could last well past the time Pen and Zach were to take the mic.

August in Illinois was hot, but nothing like Texas hot. There wasn't much fresh air to be had on the balcony, but it was private, and she desperately needed a break from the fake smiles. Her cheeks were starting to ache.

Sweltering heat, even this late in the day, blanketed her bare shoulders. Hot, yes, but quiet. She rested her hands on the railing and looked out at the city beyond. Of all the goals for a fresh start she'd made when she left Chicago, none of them had involved a giant engagement ring on her finger, a billionaire fiancé and a baby due by Christmas.

The phrase "Man plans and God laughs" flitted through her brain, but she could admit she was laughing with Him. True, she hadn't planned any of this, but

she was also so incredibly grateful to be pregnant—
something she likely never would've planned.

Her eyes tracked to the windows and she spotted
Zach, dark slacks accentuating his height, button-down
pale blue shirt unable to hide his muscular build.

Her heart did what it'd been doing for a few weeks
now, and gave an almost painful squeeze. She'd fallen
for him. Head over heels. Ass over teakettle. Hook,
line and sinker.

No matter how hard she tried to compartmentalize
her feelings from the relationship, they managed to glob
together into one four-letter word.

Love.

Whenever he walked into a room, she lit up. She sank
into him whenever he pulled her close for a kiss, like
she could fuse her very being with his. But all of this
oneness and overwhelming feeling of rightness wasn't
shared by her betrothed.

Zach offered support, loyalty and means but not love.
Love for his daughter? Most definitely. But for Pen,
his caring stopped at friendship, and some days before
that. Since she'd learned about his ex, Lonna, it was like
she could visibly spot each and every boundary line he
drew. Those boundaries were intentional—whether he
was aware he was doing it or not.

He took care of her, provided for her every need
and was adamant about not missing a moment of his
daughter's life. Zach made love to Penelope with a
single-minded focus on her pleasure, and if she were
a fresh-faced twentysomething, she might mistake his
actions for love.

But as a thirtysomething who'd been around the pro-verbial block a few times, she knew better.

He gave and gave and gave…everything but his heart. That part of his anatomy was walled off so solidly, she hadn't managed to breach the outer layer. And if she noticed the distance between them—her besotted, and him casually comfortable—so would his family, even-tually. And so would their daughter.

Pen had made a lot of decisions recently—big, sweeping life decisions—and the number-one decision she'd made was to put her daughter first.

She would sacrifice anything—her job, her home, her very lifestyle—to give her daughter what she needed. She'd even sacrifice what she had with Zach. And that was saying something as it was the first time she'd truly been in love.

In the quiet, dark corners of her mind lay a flickering hope that Zach might come around. That he might open up and learn to love her. The optimist in her thought he might, but the realist in her couldn't risk what it meant if he never did.

She wasn't waiting around for him to decide to love her. Not with their daughter watching. And that was why she also couldn't let the engagement continue. Sure, there'd be a stir of interest and a touch of gossip, but she could spin their interest toward their daughter. She was the reason for the relationship anyway. Most of it.

Some of it, Pen sadly corrected.

Regardless, percentages didn't matter. Penelope didn't want her love for Zach to grow bitter and stale after years of not being returned. More important, she didn't want her daughter to witness her mother's feelings for her father crumbling into dust.

Their daughter would have a mother and a father who cared about one another, who respected one another. Who loved her with all their hearts. And that was going to have to be enough. For all of them.

Zach must've escaped the clutches of his grandparents' friends, because he now stood at the balcony door with Chase. They were talking, looking very much like brothers with the same strong lines of their backs and hands buried in pants pockets.

Zach chose that moment to look over and catch her eye. He didn't smile, but held her gaze with a smoldering one of his own. His longish hair was tickling the collar of his shirt, his full mouth flinching in displeasure.

As magnanimous as she'd sounded in her own ears moments ago, Pen's heart throbbed with the need to satisfy her own desires rather than her daughter's.

She only wished loving Zach satisfied both.

Nineteen

Zach took in Pen on the balcony, observing her as he had when he'd first laid eyes on her. A white lace dress hugged every inch of her, from exquisite breasts to shapely hips. The graceful line of her neck led to pale blue eyes that could stop a man dead in his tracks—and full lips that had stopped his heart for at least one beat on several occasions.

Now, knowing her the way he did, he still appreciated her physical attributes, but what he mostly saw was beauty. Beauty in a dress that showed off what women at the party kept referring to as her "baby bump." Beauty, decadently outlined in white lace, snatching away first place from the breathtaking sunset behind her.

Beauty that was all woman.

That was all his.

Was. That word punched him in the solar plexus so hard, the room around him seemed to cant. He'd been possessive over her since the beginning, not wanting to let her go.

And now she was going.

Pen played with a few strands of her hair that had come down from an elegant twist at the back of her neck, her other hand resting on the railing. Her red shoes had tall, spindly heels, in spite of how many times he'd asked her not to wear them.

Throughout the evening, his flared temper had died down. His thoughts, while meeting guests who were his parents' friends more than his, kept returning to Penelope and his unborn child. His future.

Not only his future.

Theirs.

He envisioned his daughter's birthdays. Holidays. Family vacations.

As he'd glimpsed each fractured bit, he realized it was an impermanent, if not impossible, future.

Because Penelope was backing away from him.

There was no escaping how much she'd infiltrated his life in a short period of time. Zach barely recognized himself from the man who'd smoothly followed her back to her apartment for what was supposed to be a hell of a one-night stand.

And tonight it was ending.

Pen turned and caught his gaze, only to face the city lights once again. Over his shoulder, Chase spoke, and Zach wrenched his attention away from her.

"You've done it, haven't you?" Chase asked, expression serious.

Zach threw back his champagne and wished it was beer. He had a good idea of what his brother was referring to, but damned if he was about to guess.

"The pretending has become real."

"The pretending," Zach said, relinquishing his empty glass to a nearby table, "is about to come to an end." At Chase's frown, Zach explained in a low voice so no one could overhear. "The engagement is over."

"Why?"

"Why?" Zach practically spat the word. "Weren't you the one advising me not to get in too deep because I thought this would be 'fun'?"

"Yes."

Their silent standoff ended with Chase explaining.

"It's become clear to me that she means a lot more than a good time to you. So again, I ask, why?"

Zach blinked, his brother's stern visage blurring as Stef's voice crackled over the speakers in the room.

"Five minutes until we learn whether I have a niece or a nephew!"

The crowd clapped, and there were a few titters of excitement.

"If you don't know, you'd better figure it out in five minutes," Chase recommended. Zach followed his brother's gaze to Penelope and the world wasn't just canting but *swimming*.

"If you were going to succumb to a woman—" Chase nodded his head in greeting when Pen turned to look at them "—that'd be the one to lie down for."

"I've tried," Zach mumbled through numb lips. She was the one ending it. He was the one who wanted to keep her close.

"Try harder." One more cocky tilt of his lips and Chase was gone.

Rather than make another excuse that he had tried, Zach considered that maybe he hadn't. That maybe a fake engagement wasn't enough for the woman who spelled out future with a capital *F*.

Like the F *dangling from the bracelet on her wrist.*

His. Pen was still his. She needed to know that the engagement he'd thrown out as a distraction had become real for him. That was what Chase had meant when he'd told Zach to try harder.

Decisively, and damn that felt better than uncertainty, Zach slid the balcony door aside and stepped out into the heated air with his fiancée.

"Is it time?" Her tone was neutral, her body held in check. She was ready to unravel everything at that microphone, and Zach had about two minutes to stop her from doing it.

"We have to talk."

Her fair eyebrows lifted. "Didn't I get in trouble for saying something similar to you before?"

He didn't break stride, reaching her in a few steps and cradling her elbow. The deep hues of a purple-and-pink sky had given way to ink-blue.

"We have to talk about the announcement," he said, throat tight, sweat beading on his forehead, and *not* from the summer temperatures. He wasn't at the mercy of his nerves—not ever. Not when he proposed to Lonna years ago, or when he proposed to his ex-wife in Vegas, but now that he was faced with proposing to Penelope, there was no other word for it.

He was nervous.

Not only did he have no idea if she'd say yes, but he was almost positive she'd say no.

He needed her not to say no.

Not just for him. For herself—for their daughter. For all of them.

"Penelope Brand." He cleared his throat, the seriousness in his tone causing her lips to softly part. He lifted her left hand and thumbed the engagement ring he'd placed there on a whim. Or some kind of mental dare. Now that he knew her inside and out, and knowing she'd bear his first child, he knew better.

It might have started out as a whim, but now? He meant it.

"I know what we have started out as fake, but over the past several months, having you at my side, being with you day in and day out... The announcement that you were pregnant, learning we're expecting a daughter..." He trailed off, the magnitude of what they'd shared stealing his breath. "The reality is, Penelope—" he locked his gaze on her startled one "—this isn't fake. Not anymore."

"Zach..."

"Let me finish."

His eyebrows closed over his nose in concentration as the second hand rapidly ticked away precious minutes. Quickly, he reordered his thoughts. Now to deliver them in the most genuine, efficient way possible.

"We're good together," he told her. "Not only in the bedroom. As a unit. We're learning our way, and I probably have further to go than you do, but we're committed to the same important goal. Raising our child surrounded by so much love she'll never want for anything."

Pen's eyes filled and she blinked. In her expression, Zach saw hope—hope that gave him the courage to continue.

"I love our daughter with a fierceness I didn't know was possible. I care about you, Penelope. I don't want to end what we have because your PR timeline says we should."

Her expression blanked. He couldn't tell if she was shocked or in agreement, or if she felt equal measures of both.

He thumbed her diamond engagement ring so that it was centered on her finger. Then he looked her dead in the eye and forced past his constricting throat, "Will you marry me? For real this time."

In the space of one heartbeat, then two, Pen only stared. Then her lips firmed, tears streaked down her cheeks and she tugged her hand away from his.

Pen swiped her tears away almost angrily as the city melted in her watery vision. She sucked in a gulp of air, calling upon her very strong constitution for assistance. Her heart was cracked when she'd arrived.

Zach had just shattered it.

He moved to comfort her instantly, his wide, warm hands on her hips, strong chest flanking her back.

"Pen. I know how this sounds. I know you think it's too late…"

But that wasn't it. This wasn't about timing.

I love our daughter. I care about you.

He couldn't have been any clearer about the division of his feelings—about the clearly marked boundary lines—during his proposal.

She'd believed when he'd started his speech that miraculously, she'd broken through. That during the course of this party, Zach had seen the light.

I love our daughter. I care about you.

His was a marriage proposal of convenience the first time, and now it was one of merged interests. It hadn't come from his heart and soul. A long time ago she'd convinced herself she didn't need romantic love. But now that she was looking at Zach, her heart twisting like a wrung-out cloth, she was certain about two things.

One, she loved him, and two, she refused to enter a marriage where Zach was only half in.

He might never leave her, cheat on her, or abandon her, but he also wouldn't ever love her the way she deserved to be loved.

And she *deserved* love.

He stood behind her, his breath on her ear when he bent forward. "I know I'm springing this on you, but this is the best plan. We can have each other, have our daughter, have our lives together."

She closed her eyes against the surge of longing in her chest. There was a part of her, and it wasn't small, that wanted to turn in the circle of his arms and say *yes*.

Give in to the idea that Zach might someday love her the way she loved him.

But that was a fairy tale. Her life wasn't glass slippers and godmothers. It was pumpkins and practicality.

She turned and faced him, shoulders back, chin tipped to take in his handsome face, and spoke in her most practical voice. "We can't be this selfish because we like to have sex, Zach."

His head jerked on his neck like she'd slapped him instead of spoken.

"What the hell's that supposed to mean?" he bit out.

"It means exactly what I said. We have a child to think about."

"A child who needs both of her parents around," he said, his voice escalating, "not one at a time at pre-arranged intervals."

"Our child needs parents who love her and love each other. If we can't fulfill both of those bare minimums, then we have nothing more to talk about."

"Marriage isn't good enough for you?" Zach's cheeks reddened. "Marriage *and* sex isn't good enough for you?" His voice was measured and low, but anger outlined every word.

"Is it good enough for you?"

"Marriage and sex and you? Damn straight it's good enough. What more do you want from me, Penelope?"

She parted her lips to tell him there was so, *so* much more to want. So much more to marriage apart from sex and sharing a house. She and Zach could be so much more than parents. What about when their daughter was raised and out of the house? What about Penelope's *own* life beyond being a mother? What about that deep, committed love she'd seen in her parents' lives? Didn't he want that?

"The original agreement was to untangle these knots *before* our baby was born. And that's what we're doing." She started for the balcony door, but Zach caught her upper arm and tugged her back.

In his face, she saw a plethora of emotion. Pain. Fear. Anger. Hope.

As per his usual, he went with his standby: demanding.

"I can't let you do that. I'm far from done exploring what we have. Sharing what we've built."

She shook out of his grip. "What we *have* is built on a lie and an accident!"

The moment she lifted her voice to shout the accusation, his eyes slid over her shoulder and the sound of low, casual chatter filtered out onto the balcony.

Reason being, Stefanie Ferguson stood at the threshold to the balcony, door open wide. Her eyes welled with unshed tears, betrayal radiating off her strong, petite form.

"Stefanie," Pen started, but Stef steeled her spine and looked, not to Penelope, but to Zach for answers.

"Is that true?" Stef asked him.

Behind her, onlookers peered out, eyebrows raised, mouths forming *O*s of curiosity. Stef shut the door behind her and stepped onto the patio, crossing her arms over her midsection.

"What lie?" she asked.

"Stef," Pen tried again, but the younger woman stood in front of her brother. Zach, who'd released Pen the moment Stefanie appeared, shoved his hands into his pockets.

"Penelope and I are discussing something very important. Go inside and we'll be in soon."

"Tell me what lie and I'll leave you to it," Stef said.

"I said—"

"The engagement isn't real," Pen blurted. Zach's jaw clenched and he shot Pen a look showcasing both his outrage and feelings of betrayal. Well, too bad. She felt betrayed, too.

Pen took her eyes off him to comfort her almost-future-sister-in-law, who looked thoroughly heartbroken.

"Zach made up the engagement when Yvonne interrupted Chase's birthday party," Pen said softly. "He needed a distraction."

"And you agreed." Stef's voice was steel, similar to the tone her brother had used many times before.

"I agreed to help him, yes." Pen thrust her chin forward. She hadn't done anything wrong.

"And the pregnancy?" Mortification colored Stef's features as she swept her eyes to Pen's belly. "Is it real?"

"Yes." Pen let out a gusty sigh. "God. Yes, Stefanie. I'd never lie about that. I was pregnant the night of Chase's birthday party, but didn't know it."

Stef's sigh of relief was short-lived. "You lied to me." She swung her gaze from Pen to include Zach. "Both of you."

"It started out as a lie to distract from Yvonne, yes," Zach said. "But things between Pen and me have developed since then." He fastened his eyes on Penelope, but spoke to his sister. "I proposed to Pen right before you walked out here."

The warm breeze lifted Stefanie's bangs from her forehead. She tightened her arms around her middle and shook her head.

"I don't think your proposal went over well." Stef backed to the door. "I came out here to tell you we're ready for the announcement about the baby…" Inside a sea of curious faces studied the scene beyond the wide windows. Pen and Zach and Stef must look like a dramatic silent movie from their guests' vantage point. "Now it seems you owe your guests an explanation.

"Tell them the truth, Zach," Stef said. "It's the least you could've done for me." She pulled open the door but before she went inside, skewered Pen with, "I expected it from him. Not from you."

Once she was inside, Chase pushed out the door next and angled his head at his brother.

"Excuse me." Penelope bumped past Chase's suited arm and darted through the crowd. Zach called her name, but when she peeked over her shoulder, Chase was blocking the door and giving advice she knew Zach didn't want to hear.

"Let her go."

Twenty

Zach muscled past his brother. Or tried anyway. Chase, despite his suit and community standing, pushed *back*.

He banded an arm around Zach, which might look like he was consoling his younger brother, but felt more like he was attempting to crush Zach's ribs until they audibly snapped.

Through his teeth, Chase said, "Hold it together," as he shut the door to the balcony behind them. "We're outside having a brotherly chat."

Chase released him and pulled his shoulders back and Zach mirrored his stance. Inside family and friends dashed concerned looks to the balcony and then in the direction Penelope had left.

"You have thirty seconds. I'm not going to stand out here when I should be going after her."

"Stefanie went after her. Didn't you see?" Chase replied calmly. Years of experience in the public eye had made him adept at handling a crisis situation with ease. "If Pen wanted to talk to you, she'd still be standing on this balcony. Everyone inside is waiting for an announcement. Granted, they got one, but it wasn't the one they were expecting."

Zach thrust his hand into his hair. Of course it hadn't been what they were expecting. Pen's reaction to his proposal hadn't been what *he* was expecting.

"Your options," Chase continued, "are to either leave and let the gossip begin. Or stay and offer a generic explanation."

"Like what?"

"If it were me? I'd apologize with no more explanation than a 'my fault.'" Chase demonstrated with his hands in surrender pose.

"*My* fault," Zach growled. "*My fault?* It's my fault for asking Penelope to marry me? For asking the woman carrying my baby to stay with me the rest of our lives?"

"Lower your voice."

"You're as bad as the rest of them, Chase. I don't give a fuck about public opinion or what anyone in that room needs."

"Yes, that's clear." Chase reprimanded in an irritatingly calm tone. "You only care about one person. *You*."

That was it. He'd had it. Had it with trying to do the right thing and being crucified for it.

"You know what?" Zach shouldered by Chase and gripped the handle to the door. "Tell them whatever the hell you want."

* * *

"Penelope! Wait."

Pen paused on the sidewalk, surprised that Stefanie had followed her down. Stef had been clear upstairs that she didn't appreciate being left in the dark.

"Where are you going?" the younger woman called as she clipped to a stop next to Pen.

"You were right in there. You deserved to know. I'm sorry I didn't tell you. I couldn't."

"You should be. I'm mad at you and my idiot brother for keeping a secret this huge from me. I kept your pregnancy to myself! I could've kept this quiet, too." Stefanie stepped closer, kindness in her eyes. "But no matter how mad I am, I'd still give you a ride home."

Pen folded her arms over her middle, the reality of her situation settling in. She didn't have a home…only the home she shared with Zach. "I don't want to go home."

Not tonight. Maybe never again. This was as good of a break as any. Her leaving had always been inevitable. From the first time she spotted Zach in Chicago, to the jazz club, to the morning he kissed her goodbye, some part of her knew that holding on to him would be like trying to hold on to the wind.

Maybe getting it over with would allow her to heal quickly.

She hoped.

"I won't ask you to choose between me and your brother," Pen told Stef, because she refused to be unfair.

"I'm not *choosing*." Stefanie dug through her clutch.

"I'm helping out a friend. If that makes Zach mad, so be it."

Stefanie approached the valet with her ticket. "We're in a hurry."

"Yes, ma'am," the valet replied with a hat-tip. Then he ran—yes, *ran*—to get the car.

Sadly, not fast enough.

This time when Penelope heard her name, it was Zach. He slowed his jog when he was close, brow pinched and fists bunched.

"I'm taking her home with me," Stefanie stated.

"No, you're not."

Stef turned on him. "Yes. I am."

"Pen." In his eyes, Penelope saw the plea. A dab of pain that hadn't been there before. But she couldn't open up again, not after what it took to get to this point.

"I have nothing more to discuss, Zach," Pen announced sadly. "You offered me everything and nothing at the same time."

His mouth froze open for a moment before clacking shut. Baring his teeth, he said, "I offered you everything I could."

She swallowed past a thick throat as the valet pulled Stef's car to the curb. Through a watery, sad smile, she nodded. "I know. And it's not enough."

Zach, arms folded, watched one of the movers walk the last of Penelope's boxes downstairs before loading the box into a moving truck.

He wasn't one for admitting defeat, but with Penelope

standing in the hallway, notebook in hand as she checked off a list, it was clear they were over.

"What about the baby stuff?" the other mover asked, pointing to the room behind Zach.

Pen turned, her white summer dress rounded at the front, her heeled sandals reasonably high for a change.

"Yes," Zach answered at the same time Penelope said, "No."

Their gazes clashed, and in her pale blue eyes, he saw both challenge and loss. Or maybe he felt it.

"Take it," he told her.

"You'll need it," she said with a head-shake.

"I can buy more." He could replace every single thing in this house with a phone call, save one. The blonde across from him on the landing.

He'd tried contacting her for the past few days, but after the one night she slept at Stef's, he hadn't been able to reach her. Even Pen's office had been dark when he stopped by.

Then, this morning she'd texted him to ask if he'd be home. Foolishly, he'd believed she was coming by to reconcile. Instead, she'd shown up driving ahead of a moving truck.

So this was it.

She'd made up her mind. She was leaving.

"I can buy more, too, Zach. I have time before she's born. And anyway, I'm not sure how much of the furniture I can fit in my apartment."

His chest tightened as his eyes dipped to Pen's stomach. He was losing…everything. And it flat-out pissed him off.

"Are we going to talk about this?" he all but shouted. A mover leaned on the wall outside the bedroom door to watch. Oh, hell no. Zach curled his lip when he addressed him. "Get the hell out of my house."

He went, ambling down the stairs, and bitching to his friend who stood on the porch. But both men stayed outside.

Zach turned back to Pen. "Well?"

"Well, what? There's nothing to talk about." She gestured with her notebook. "I've decided. Luckily, my landlady loves me and ushered me into the first available two-bedroom she had."

"You had the space you needed here." He widened his arms to encompass the massive house he now lived in alone.

"I never asked for this," she replied. He wished she would've yelled. Her maintaining her composure made him wonder if she cared about him at all.

"There are arrangements to be made," he growled, hating the loss of control, the feeling of spinning out of it. "Decisions about our daughter."

"Yes." She flipped to the back of the notebook, tore out a sheet of paper and handed it to him. "They've been made. Consider this a proposal. We can define the particulars later."

Penelope the Planner had an answer for everything. He folded his arms rather than take the sheet of paper.

"Why are you doing this really?" he asked.

"Because." She sighed. "As much as you claim to know what you want—" she tucked the paper back into her notebook "—you deserve better than an arranged marriage with a child as the prize."

Her smile was sad when she finished with, "And so do I."

Stepping close to him, she placed her hand on his chest, went up on her toes and placed a brief kiss on the corner of his mouth. Too brief. When he moved to hold her, she backed away.

"We'll be okay," she promised. Her eyes went to the baby's room. "Keep the furniture. You'll need it for when she visits."

Pen walked downstairs, calling out to the movers, "We're done here, guys. I'll follow in my car."

Zach's screen door shut with a bang behind her as car and truck engines turned over and pulled out of the driveway. He lowered to the top step upstairs, elbows on his knees and listened to the quiet of the house.

There was defeat in the silence.

Zachary Ferguson didn't do defeat.

He stood, in that instant deciding he'd do whatever it took to win Penelope back. To make her understand what she was walking away from. To make crystal clear that the best path for their future was a future with him in it.

He had a few billion in the bank.

Surely he could come up with something.

Twenty-One

Pen's mother sprayed the dusting cloth with Pledge and wiped the rungs of a wooden crib. Paula and Louis had driven to Texas, claiming the road trip would do them good. They'd arrived the day after the movers left everything behind and Pen had been so glad to see them, she could've cried.

In fact, she had.

"It was yours when you were a baby," her mother said as she polished the crib. "I honestly didn't remember that we had it. Your father cleaned out the storage unit and there it was."

"Thank you, Mom."

Paula Brand abandoned her work and scooped Pen into a hug with just the right amount of pressure. Pen would have cried more if there were any tears left.

"Are you going to tell me the real reason behind you walking out on your billionaire fiancé?" Her mom held her at arm's length and waited.

Pen's lips compressed as she considered doing just that. She was willing to tell her mother a partial truth, but she couldn't bear confessing that the engagement was never real. Especially since, for Pen, her love for Zach was *very* real.

"When Zach proposed—" *both times* "—he did it out of obligation rather than love. I couldn't settle for less than his whole heart." Speaking of heart, hers gave a mournful wail. Walking out on him instead of accepting half measures was harder than she'd like to believe.

She'd been comfortable with him. She had a home, combined parenting, and yes, the money was a source of comfort, as well. But she wasn't the type of woman to let comfort and stability rule her world. If she were, she never would've left Chicago.

Hand resting on her swollen stomach, Pen thanked God that she had left Chicago. That she carried this baby in her belly and that, for all the heartache Zach had caused her, she'd finally experienced love.

"I'm sorry, sweetheart." Paula shook her head and let out an exasperated sigh. "I wish I could share a story so I could relate, but the truth is I was lucky to find your father when I was young."

Penelope's parents were high school sweethearts who married and built a business and had a baby because they were ready. Not because, in the midst of finding companionship, the birth control hadn't worked. But she didn't begrudge them their happiness.

"I'm glad you can't relate," she told her mother with a smile.

"Regardless, life is not without its struggles." Paula palmed her daughter's cheeks and returned her smile.

"I'll be fine. I've picked myself up and dusted myself off more times than I can count." Pen felt like bawling, but she was going to have to buck up. She wanted her daughter to be as proud of her as Pen was of her own mother.

Pen had done the unthinkable—she'd fallen for a guy who was unwilling to share his heart. His world, his money, yes. But not his heart. And in the end, that was all she'd wanted.

"I have something for you." Paula went to her purse and came out with an envelope. A very flat envelope. "We had an unexpected windfall after that last house flip—"

"Mom, no." Pen backed away like her mother held a live spider by the leg rather than an envelope by the corner.

"Your dad and I want you to have this. We're going to be grandparents. We want to start our spoiling early." She shook the envelope. "I mean it."

Pen accepted it with a murmured "Thank you."

Paula rubbed her hands together. "I can't wait to go shopping for this baby!"

Pen thought of the Love & Tumble boutique, of the photographer she'd hired and the Dallas Duchess blog. She'd avoided much of the handling of her own potential PR nightmare for the last week-plus. She didn't care about her reputation—none of it was career-altering—

but there were elements to handle that affected the Fergusons.

The mayor.

Stefanie.

Zach.

Penelope resolved to handle them as soon as possible.

"I don't know what to say," Pen said, holding the envelope in both hands. Blank on the outside, and who knew how much money on the inside. It didn't matter. What mattered was that her parents were supportive of her decision to raise her child apart from Zach, and that they loved her no matter what.

Anything beyond that involved items on Pen's own to-do list. Items like shared custody and drop-offs. Announcing the sex of the baby as well as confirming the breakup for the public.

"I'm going to run to work, if that's okay?" She phrased it like a question but knew her mother's response before she gave it.

"That a girl." Paula smiled proudly.

In her downtown office, Pen sat at her desk and jotted a quick list of phone calls to make, pausing to mourn the space. She'd have to abandon her office to work at home. Start having meetings in coffee shops and her clients' offices again. She could no longer afford both Brand Consulting's shingle and her daughter.

Hand on her tummy, she closed her eyes and reminded herself of what was important.

Then she picked up her desk phone and called the mayor of Dallas.

* * *

Chase showed up in Zach's office five minutes before five o'clock, a shadow of the same hour decorating his jaw.

"You look like shit," Zach offered. "Rough day?"

Chase held his gaze but didn't cop to the status of his day, instead returning, "I'd talk. You look like your rough days had friends who came by to beat the hell out of you at night."

"Wonder why that is." Zach blinked tired eyes. He hadn't been sleeping well. Or eating well. Or thinking well, either. Suffering from a breakup would do that. And he did mean *suffering.*

"Penelope called me this afternoon," Chase said.

That snapped Zach awake. "You? Why?"

"She let me know she was announcing your amicable breakup via a blogger. Duchess something. Pen asked me to pass it on. In person."

"That was bold." No one told the mayor of Dallas what to do. "And you agreed."

"I came to tell you that and one more thing."

"Which is?" Zach asked as he typed in the URL for the Dallas Duchess. No news about himself was on the front page, but an ad for Love & Tumble caught his eye and snagged his heart.

"Penelope misses you."

Zach tore his eyes from the screen. "Did she say that?"

"She didn't have to. She sounded…sad." Chase's eyes skated over Zach's rumpled shirt. "I wonder if she looks as bad as you do. I doubt it. She's a helluva lot prettier."

No arguing that finer point.

"I can't go by your gut, Chase." But even as he said

it, Zach's mind was turning. He'd been racking his brain all week for ways to win her back.

His eyes on the blog in front of him, he considered a new possibility. Maybe he could out-PR the PR maven.

"I'm not giving up," Zach told his brother.

"It's hard to know when to give up and when to dig in." Chase's tone was contemplative. He sucked in a breath and expelled such a personal comment, Zach stared at him in shock. "Like when Mimi and I unraveled. Mom and Dad were right. She wasn't a good fit for a political partner, but at the time, I struggled. I didn't know my future. I didn't know if I'd actually make it to mayor when she left. But I knew if I did, I'd be better off without her."

Despite Chase's assuredness as he recited the tale of the decay of his past relationship, Zach had been there when it happened. He remembered his older brother's state when he lost Mimi. He'd been devastated for months. Then again, devastation on Chase looked different than it did on other people. Chase had dug his heels in and honed his focus on world domination.

He'd fallen just short of the world, but he'd landed Dallas. Zach wasn't sure if his stiff-lipped older brother was a good template with which to map out his own future or not.

"The point is you need to figure out what you want your life to look like in five, ten, twenty years," Chase said. "What role does Penelope play? She's the mother of your child, but is marrying her really what's best for you? Or is the best thing for you to back away from her and let the future fall into place?"

As Chase spoke, Zach rose from his chair.

"Are you kidding me right now? This is the advice you're offering? You don't know what Pen and I were like together. When she was in my house. In my *life*." When she was settled across from him in a restaurant, laughing over her wine. Or in the doctor's office, with tears of joy shining in her eyes. Or when she'd moved out of his house with such resolve, that Zach questioned whether or not he'd imagined her every reaction beforehand.

"Simple question," Chase said in his typical uber-calm state. "She misses you. Do you miss her?"

More than anyone knew.

"Yes."

"Do you love her?" Since the inflection and volume of Chase's voice hadn't changed even a little, Zach had to let that question settle into the pit of his gut.

His churning, uncertain, fear-filled gut.

"There's your answer," Chase said. "Let her go, Zach. Love, even when it's real and lasting, isn't a sure thing. But when it's not there, you're betting on a loss. The longer you let a loveless relationship go on, the bigger that loss is."

On that note, Chase gave him a curt nod and left the office.

Twenty-Two

Pen stepped into her building and the woman positioned at the front desk waved her over. "This came for you, Ms. Brand."

Oh, no. Not again.

Penelope pasted a smile on her face and accepted a padded envelope…and then another one.

"One more," the woman said, handing over a small box. She eyed Pen's rounded tummy. "I can carry these up if it's too much for you."

"No, I have them." The packages were awkward, especially while juggling her purse and working the elevator, but they weren't heavy.

Upstairs she dropped everything on a chair in her living room and stared at the packages in contemplation.

The return address was Love & Tumble. She'd re-

ceived packages from there every day—several of them.
So far, they'd been the items she'd had Zach's assistant
return to the store right after they'd purchased them.
Zach had tried to talk her into keeping them but of
course, she hadn't. Now, one by one, or in this case
three by three, those same items they'd returned had
been showing up on her doorstep.

She opened the envelopes. One held a onesie, the
other a baby blanket. The smaller box required scissors
to cut the tape, so Penelope took the box to the counter-
top and grabbed her kitchen shears.

Inside the box, wrapped in Love & Tumble's signature shimmer-green tissue paper, was a pair of shoes.
But not just any pair of shoes. Blinged out, faux fur,
rhinestone encrusted high-top tennies for a girl.

Pen batted her lashes, fighting tears. This wasn't
something she'd purchased prior. She and Zach had
looked at this pair in the store and she'd mentioned if
she had a girl, she'd *never* buy her six-hundred-dollar
shoes. He'd argued that if they learned they were having a girl, those would be the *first* pair he'd buy her.

And he had.

A tear streaked Pen's cheek as she thumbed the tiny
soles. Zach had been trying to buy back her affection
since she left with the movers. He was being very sweet.
Very thoughtful.

As the father of her child, she couldn't have picked
a better man to love her baby more.

But he still didn't love *her*.

She hated how right she'd been in saying no to his
proposal. He'd proposed to keep their budding family

together, which was honorable, and for some women might have been enough. Still, when she imagined Zach or her marrying other people, Pen's heart ached with loss.

A swift knock at the door jolted her out of her thoughts. One glance at the clock reminded her what she already knew. This morning Stefanie had texted to ask if she could swing by tonight. Pen had texted back yes, then phoned the front desk telling them to send her up when she arrived.

She swiped the hollows of her eyes and shook off her somber attitude, then rushed to open the door. Stef stood at the entry, her bright smile fading as soon as she got one look at Pen.

"Oh, my gosh. What happened now?" Zach's sister pushed her way into the apartment, her hands wrapping around Pen's shoulders.

Rather than explain, Pen gestured around the apartment. At the pile of boxes she'd been meaning to break down for recycling. At another pile of their contents: baby clothes and toys and blankets, taking up the length of the sofa. She lost her battle holding back tears. "Your brother mails me gifts every day."

"That jerk," Stefanie said.

Pen let out a startled laugh, but Stef didn't laugh with her.

"Has he come to see you?"

Pen shook her head. "No, but I wouldn't want him to."

"Has he called you?"

Pen shook her head again.

"Texted?" Stef asked, her voice small.

Pen confirmed with another head shake.

Stef clucked her tongue and proffered an envelope. "This came for you, and Zach handed it to me when I barged in on him at the office."

Pen took the envelope. Her name was on the front in fanciful calligraphy, addressed to the house Zach had purchased.

"How…is he?" Pen hated herself for asking, but she couldn't not ask.

"Stressed. He looks tired. Heartbroken. About like you do." At Pen's wan smile, Stef tapped the envelope. "Expensive card stock. What do you think it is?"

Pen flipped over the envelope where there was a return address in black block letters, but no name.

"Not sure." Pen tore open the back and pulled out a sturdy white square with a vellum overlay. In gold lettering, two names stood out. Ashton Weaver and Serena Fern. "It's a wedding invitation."

Stef snatched it back and read the invite. "The actors?"

"Yep."

"Wow. I don't get starstruck often, but *wow*."

"They'll probably make it." Pen, shoulders rounded in defeat, trudged to the couch, shoved the baby stuff aside and collapsed onto a cushion. "And then I'll have to go to their twenty-fifth anniversary party knowing that two unlikely souls made it at the same time my engagement ended."

She pulled a pillow onto her lap and squeezed. Stef made room for herself and joined Pen on the couch.

Pen had decided not to wallow. She'd decided to move on and pick up the pieces and focus on being the best mom *ever*. Her wounded heart had delayed those plans.

"I didn't mean to," Pen admitted around a sob.

"You didn't mean to what?" Stef's voice softened. She rubbed Pen's back and Pen realized abruptly how badly she'd needed a girlfriend to confide in. Stefanie was the exact wrong person to lean on. As Zach's sister, she shouldn't be forced to choose sides.

And yet, when Pen opened her mouth to say "Never mind," she said, "I fell in love with your stupid brother," instead.

"Chase?"

Pen let out a surprised bleat. Stef smirked.

"Chase is *stupid*. Zach is the *idiot*." But Stef's smile was one of concern when she continued rubbing Pen's back. "You love Zach. You're having my niece. He proposed. What's the problem?"

"Oh, you know. Just that he doesn't love me." Pen swiped her cheeks and sniffed. "He loves the idea of a family and us being together. We're super-compatible in bed." She sniffed. "Sorry if that's too much information," she mumbled when Stef wrinkled her nose in disgust.

"I'm trying to absorb it. I am." Stef sighed. "How can he not love you? *I* love you." After a brief pause, she added, "Do you want to marry me?"

Pen let out a watery laugh. "I'll be fine. No, I'll be great. It's hormones, you know? And there have been a lot of big changes lately. I'm sure it'll all shake out."

Pen gave Stef a reassuring nod, but when Zach's sis-

ter nodded back, it was obvious the youngest Ferguson
was placating her. Pen could take the placation. What
she couldn't take another second of were the tears of
regret.

"Enough of that." Pen slapped her hands to her
thighs. "Do you want to help me take the tags off my
daughter's clothes and sort them for the laundry?"

Stef's face brightened. "That, I can gladly do." With
a quick clap of her hands, she leaped off the couch, baby
clothes in hand.

Laundry was a lot better than wallowing.

The baby clothes weren't working.

Zach sent package after package from Love & Tumble,
and had yet to hear anything from Penelope. He'd have
to move on to something else.

Something *bigger*.

He'd fill her apartment with flowers. Hire a sky-
writer. Buy an island…

He didn't own an island yet.

iPad on his lap, he typed *islands for sale* into the
search engine as a red sports car growled to a stop at
the front of his house. Yeah, *the house*. He'd sworn he'd
move back into his bachelor-pad apartment, but after
Pen put the final nail in the coffin of their *us* status,
leaving felt like giving up.

He wasn't about to give up.

His sister stepped out of the car into morning sunshine and Zach met her at the door.

"You're up early."

A large pair of sunglasses suggested she was out late.

She propped them on top of her head as she came into the house, but her eyes were clear and alert.

"I was up late," she confirmed, "but pregnant ladies don't drink, so Penelope and I indulged in cookies and tea instead." She shrugged her mouth. "Not a bad way to spend a Friday night, actually."

She was at Penelope's apartment?

"How is she?" he asked without hesitation.

"Funny, she asked the same question about you." Stefanie offered a Ferguson-family smirk. "Do you have coffee?"

"I'm working my way through a pot now." He followed Stefanie into the kitchen where she poured herself a mug and offered him a refill. He set the iPad aside and retrieved his mug. When he walked back into the kitchen, Stef was frowning down at the tablet.

"You are not going to buy an island."

"Why not?" He refilled his mug.

"Are you moving there?"

"No." Although if Pen kept ignoring him, an island would be the ideal place to live. "Maybe. I don't know. I was going to buy it for Penelope."

Stefanie scowled. "Seriously, Zach."

"Seriously, Stef." He opened his mouth to argue until it belatedly occurred to him that his sister was a woman.

He didn't have a lot of women at his disposal. He had yet to poll a woman about how to move forward with *Mission: Get Pen Back*. And God knew Chase hadn't been a lot of help.

"Is skywriting a better idea?"

"Man. This is bad." Stef gave him a pitying shake of her head.

"I can buy out every flower shop downtown. Hell, I can *buy* every flower shop downtown. Is that…a better idea?" He palmed the back of his neck and leaned a hip on the counter. He was completely out of his element. "She didn't respond to the baby clothes."

"I'm not sure this is a situation you can buy yourself out of, Zach. If you didn't have billions in the bank, what would you do?"

He drank his coffee. Partially to buy time and partially because the caffeine might help him think.

"If you couldn't *name a planet* after her, what would you do?"

"A planet. Hand me that iPad."

Stef narrowed her eyes in warning.

"I'm kidding. I feel like you're dancing around a point."

"Why are you doing all of this?"

"I'm winning her back." *Duh*. Wasn't that obvious? "We're good together and as soon as I can get her to stop ignoring the truth…"

"Which is?"

He blinked at his sister. What the hell was that supposed to mean?

"Why are you good together, Zach?" she pressed.

He frowned. "What do you mean *why*?"

"How do you feel about her?"

He let out an uncomfortable laugh and pushed away from the counter. "How do I feel… That's obvious, isn't it? I want her around. I want to raise our daughter together."

Stefanie sat down at the breakfast bar and pilfered a cookie from an open bag. "Why?" she asked around a bite.

"Pen's fun. She gets me." And in the bedroom? Forget it. There wasn't a high enough rating for how explosive they were when they came together.

"What else?" Stef cocked her head.

"I…miss her." That hurt to admit.

"And?"

"And what?" He put down his mug before he sloshed hot coffee on his arm. Flattening both hands on the bar, he bent to look his sister in the eyes. "Spell it out."

"Sorry." Stef polished off her cookie and dusted her hands together, not the least bit sorry. "Can't. This is heart stuff not head stuff, and Lord only knows what you're feeling in there. Do you have feelings?"

She pretended to study the ceiling as she contemplatively chewed.

"I have too many feelings. I'm drowning in feelings! Can't you see that? I'm willing to turn over my entire life. To get married!"

"You were married to a crazy person last year. Why is Pen different?"

"That was…" He swallowed thickly, on the verge of admitting the truth for the first time ever. "That was a test."

"A test *marriage*?"

"A test to make sure I could marry and it could mean nothing." Damn. He hadn't meant to be *that* honest.

"So marrying Pen would be nothing?" his sister asked gently.

"Marrying Pen would mean everything." That same jittery fear he felt when he spoke to Chase about her returned, spreading through his chest like wildfire.

Stef waited for him to say more. Could he? Could he admit what was quaking in his gut? What was making his head spin?

"She's…the mother of my child," he started. Lamely. "There's more."

Chin propped in hand, Stef waited.

"She's…" He closed his eyes and then reopened them. Screw it. The truth was obvious to Stef, so he might as well tell her what she already knew. "I'm in love with her."

Stef burst off the stool and thrust both arms into the air.

"Yesssss!" She strangled him with a hug.

He smiled against her hair, and embraced his sister. His chest filled to the brim with a feeling of *right*. That ball-zinging surety that had been eluding him—or maybe he'd been denying it for some time now.

He just as quickly deflated.

The sad reality was that he was in love with Penelope and she wanted nothing to do with him.

"She'll never come back to you if you keep showering her with gifts. You have to make a big statement," Stef said. "And trust me, I want her back almost as much as you do." Stef was on the move, her hand lashed around Zach's wrist. "There has to be some clue in this house as to how to go about getting her back."

"She took everything that was hers out of this house," he said as he allowed Stef to drag him room to room. He followed her up the stairs where she made the same sad assessment he had for days in a row.

There was no sign of Penelope here.

Other than the baby's room, it was like she hadn't been here at all.

Stef turned from the Dallas Cowboys decorations Zach hadn't bothered taking down. He'd meant to, but again, that felt like giving up.

He expected his sister to shrug and state that he was a lost cause, but instead a slow grin spread across her lips.

She grabbed his arm and gave him a shake. "I figured it out. I know how you can win her back."

Twenty-Three

Now that the other bedroom in her apartment housed a crib and a changing table, and Pen had let her office go, she'd taken to working from the sofa. She spread her planner, cell phone and laptop on the coffee table: command central. It was perfect, really, since she was only a few yards away from the coffeepot she couldn't wait to utilize again, and the bathroom.

Okay, so it wasn't perfect.

She missed her office. She needed a designated space. Once her daughter was born, she'd be home fulltime— Pen had almost convinced herself that working from home was the best-case scenario.

Until she went mad from being housebound. Then she'd have to…she didn't know what.

At least she'd landed a new account on Monday.

Bridget Baxter, a chirpy, adorable blonde had requested Pen meet her for coffee. Bridget had been referred by Serena, and had a little PR problem of her own. Pen learned that Bridget, who co-managed the Dallas Cowboys, had had a one-night stand with one of the players. She was worried he'd ruin her reputation with the team, and she didn't want to lose her high-up position. Bridget explained she'd worked hard to prove she was qualified.

Pen could *so* relate to having her reputation ruined by a man. She could also understand how Bridget had blindly followed her heart and had wound up at a destination she hadn't foreseen. Pen didn't hesitate accepting the job.

A job that smacked of her recently annihilated relationship, but also gave her something better to focus on than attempting to heal her heart, which had a million tiny lacerations.

Or maybe she was being dramatic.

The reminder for Bridget's appointment popped up on the laptop screen. Pen needed to leave soon if she expected to arrive at the stadium on time.

She'd given a lot of thought to Bridget's situation. How to best utilize the media, if at all. The more she turned it over, the angrier she became. Why was it up to Bridget to save her job? The guy she slept with certainly wasn't in danger of being ousted from the team because he slept with an executive.

It was all so unfair.

Life was unfair.

The team was practicing today, which was why Bridget wanted to meet there. That was where her former beau would be, and she wanted to pull him in on the conversation if needed.

After winding around a bunch of corridors and walking into the wrong office, Pen stopped a coach-looking guy wearing a cap and holding a clipboard, and asked for her client.

"Bridget Baxter?" he repeated, regarding Pen like she'd sprouted a horn.

"We have an appointment."

"She's practicing on the field." He shook his head. "You can follow me if you want."

She followed, her head held high. If Bridget was getting this much disrespect from the coach, Pen could imagine the uphill climb she'd have if everyone found out Bridget had slept with a guy on the team.

Determination propelled her steps out into the sticky weather where teammates and cheerleaders dotted the field.

This kind of unfairness wouldn't stand. Pen would make sure Bridget saw justice. She scanned the crowd for the tiny blonde. Ho boy. There were a *sea* of blondes in cheerleader uniforms and not a single pencil skirt in the mix.

Then one of the blondes separated from the crowd and shot Pen a wide grin.

Bridget.

Wearing a cheerleader uniform.

What?

"She's here!" Bridget shouted. In a blur of blue and silver, the cheerleaders formed a line on the field. The guys didn't stop practice, but a few of them looked at her and smiled.

Bridget bopped over to stand in front of Pen. "Sorry for the subversion. It was his plan. But I did have fun playing a corporate mogul." With a wink and a buoyant giggle, Bridget ran back to her girls.

"Whose plan?" Pen asked, confused.

"Give me a *Z*!" Bridget called out, and the cheerleaders echoed with, "*Z*!" What followed was an *A*, a *C*, and an *H*.

With each letter, Pen felt her knees weaken.

"What's that spell?" Bridget called. In answer, the cheerleaders parted, pom-poms swishing, and a tall, blond man wearing a tuxedo emerged.

Zach's hair had been recently trimmed, and his sexy dimple was in full force. Talk about input overload. The sun, the cheering, the crash of football players in the background, and in the center of it all, the very man she'd been trying to put in her rearview mirror.

"Penelope Brand," he said, looking confident and cool, and…different from before. There was sureness in each step he took toward her. Certainty in the way he dismissed the cheerleaders with a "Thanks, ladies."

"What are you doing?" Her voice was cautious for a very good reason. If he'd gone through this trouble, it was because he was making a gesture of some sort. One that didn't involve sending the UPS truck to her building every single day.

And if he asked her again to share his life with him, she didn't trust herself to tell him no. If nothing had changed in his heart, then she couldn't allow anything to change in hers.

He lifted her hand, the hand where her engagement ring used to sit. She'd left it on Zach's dresser the day she went with the movers to the house. She couldn't bear to look at it on her hand when she knew the truth behind it.

That the love she felt for Zach had ultimately not been returned.

It'd all been a ruse.

"A long time ago," he said, "I made a rule to never get hurt again."

Oh, my God, he was doing this…right here. Right now.

"Zach, please."

"You asked about Lonna. Do you want to hear the rest or not?"

She swallowed around a lump forming in her throat, curiosity and hope—so much hope it made her head spin—at a peak.

She nodded. He dipped his chin and continued.

"After I proposed to Lonna and she told me in no uncertain terms that she couldn't take me seriously, I swore I'd never fall in love again. Avoiding love was the only pathway to happiness. The only path to a fulfilled life. Or so I thought. Then I met you."

She couldn't look away from his earnest green eyes—from the sincerity in them.

"I love our daughter, Penelope, but you have to understand something." He gave her fingers a gentle squeeze. "I love her because of how much I love you."

Pen froze, eyes wide, mouth slightly ajar. Did she hear him right? She shook her head, refusing to hope. Refusing to believe.

"You're…you're… That's not true," she finished on a whisper.

"I'm not attached physically to our baby girl the way you are, Pen," he stated. "The *only* way I could feel this much love and devotion for her is because I felt it for you first. I've been in denial about this for a long time. Since the moment I proposed at my brother's birthday party."

She blinked.

"Even then, I knew." He tugged her close, locking an arm around her lower back. Between them, her swollen belly pressed against his torso.

"I love you, Penelope Brand. I'm sorry I bullied you into everything. Staying when you didn't want to stay. Moving in with me when you didn't want to give up your place. Proposing without confessing how I felt about you. It was a childish way to get what I wanted—you—without putting my heart on the line. I take it all back. I don't want you to marry me."

He didn't? She blinked, confused. That wasn't where she saw this speech headed.

"Unless," he added with a cocky smile, "you love me, too." He lifted one thick eyebrow and when she didn't respond right away, some of that certainty bled from his expression.

He wasn't sure how she felt.

Because she'd never told him.

She'd been as guilty as he was about not sharing.

She'd never given him the chance to know how she felt about him. So she'd tell him now.

"I love you so much I can't imagine my life without you." She curled her hand around one of his. "And believe me, I've been trying."

His grin was cunning, wicked with intent and promises to come. "In that case…"

He rested his teeth on his bottom lip and let out a sharp whistle. Behind him, in a flurry of movement, the cheerleaders reformed a line and held up giant white cards with letters that spelled *Marry Me?*

Zach made a circling motion with his finger and a cute redheaded cheerleader at the end flipped her card—a question mark—so that it was an exclamation point instead.

Zach faced Pen, who dropped her purse on the ground at her feet, wrapped her arms around his neck and pushed to her toes.

He sealed her mouth with his.

Behind them, cheers and whistles, and low male hollers of approval, lifted on the air as Pen allowed herself to sink into Zach's embrace.

Into the promise of his words, especially the three that meant more than anything.

He loved her.

As much as she loved him.

Epilogue

"Penelope told me she hated me," Zach announced. "Over and over."

His father, sister and brother regarded him in shocked concern. His mother, on the other hand, stood from her seat in the waiting room and let out a loud chuckle.

"Women who give birth always say that. Remember, Rider?"

"Three times," his father confirmed, standing next to his wife. "Three times I went through the birthing process at her side and she hated me every time." He pointed at Chase. "Mostly with you, though. Since you were first."

Chase and Stefanie stood from their chairs, Stef ribbing him about how it was no surprise he was the cause of the most strife of the three of them.

Zach's smile emerged—so big, it hurt his face. It'd been a relatively fast labor, but a long night. "Ready to meet her?"

Stef and his mom shrieked happy sounds, and his father and brother didn't hold back their widest grins. Zach shook his head at their attire. "I hate that she is meeting you all dressed like this, though."

"Ugly sweaters are tradition!" Stef argued, her glowing-nose-reindeer sweater one for the books.

He led his family into the room, and a collective gasp lifted on the air when they spotted the pink-wrapped bundle resting on Penelope's chest.

Pen's eyes were drooped, her hair tangled. Her own ugly sweater tossed aside on a chair with the rest of her clothing in favor of the hospital gown she now wore. She was the most beautiful sight Zach had ever seen.

Well. Second to his daughter.

"What's her name?" Elle cooed as she scooped her granddaughter into her arms. "Can you finally tell us?"

"Olivia Edna," Penelope announced with a smile. "After my grandmother, and Zach's."

His father and siblings bent over Olivia in his mother's arms. Even when handed off, Zach's daughter slept soundly.

"Your mom and dad are on their way from the airport," Zach told Pen, swiping her hair from her forehead.

Her eyes drooped sleepily, but her smile was everlasting.

He bent and placed a kiss to her forehead. "You did it."

Her pale blue eyes opened and stabbed him in the heart. How had he ever denied loving her when she was his everything?

"*We* did it," she corrected, giving him credit he hadn't earned.

A gurgle came from Olivia and she fussed in Chase's arms. Those years of holding and kissing babies must have paid off, because the mayor of Dallas bounced and shushed her and a moment later, she cooed.

Chase shot his brother a cocky smile.

"I love you," Pen whispered to Zach, reaching for his arm with her hand—a hand that boasted both a wedding band and an engagement ring. They hadn't waited. They hadn't wanted to.

Zach kissed her lips, lingering a moment. "I love you."

She played with the longer hair at his nape, in need of a trim, and whispered two words that made Zach more grateful than he'd ever been in his life.

"Merry Christmas."

Olivia was the perfect gift. Better than every wrapped present they'd left piled in his parents' living room to rush Penelope to the hospital. Better than the moment Zach spotted Penelope in the jazz club and wondered if she'd let him sample her mouth.

Better, he mused, than the moment she vowed to be with him and he with her, until death do they part.

"Uh-oh, she's had it with us," Stef announced, placing Zach's daughter in his arms.

He adjusted her so that she sank comfortably in the crook of his elbow. Looking down at the faint sweep of blond hair, puckered rosebud lips and tiny fisted hands, Zach's heart filled to capacity—who knew there was more room in there?

"Hey, Livvie," he said, his voice choked with emotion. "Merry Christmas to you, too."

* * * * *

Don't miss Chase's story, coming August 2018!

If you liked this story, pick up these other sexy billionaires from Harlequin Desire!

BILLIONAIRE'S BABY PROMISE
by Sarah M. Anderson
SNOWED IN WITH A BILLIONAIRE
by Karen Booth
MATCHED TO A BILLIONAIRE
by Kat Cantrell
BILLIONAIRE BOSS, M.D.
by Olivia Gates
THE BILLIONAIRE'S BORROWED BABY
by Janice Maynard

Available now from Harlequin Desire!

***

If you're on Twitter, tell us what you think of Harlequin Desire! #harlequindesire

Notorious playboy Nolan Madaris is determined to escape his great-grandmother's famous matchmaking schemes, but Ivy Chapman, the woman his great-grandmother has picked out for him, is nothing like he expects—and she's got her own proposal for how to get their meddling families off their backs and out of their love lives!

Read on for a sneak peek of
BEST LAID PLANS,
the latest in New York Times *bestselling author*
Brenda Jackson's
MADARIS FAMILY SAGA!

Prologue

Christmas Day

Nolan Madaris III took a sip of his beer while standing on the balcony of his condo. Leaning against the rail, he had a breathtaking view of the exclusive fifteen-story Madaris Building that was surrounded by a cluster of upscale shops, restaurants and a beautiful jogging park with a huge man-made pond. The condos where he lived were right across from the water.

The entire complex, including the condos, had been architecturally designed, engineered and constructed by the Madaris Construction Company that was owned by his cousins Blade and Slade. For the holidays, the Madaris Building and the surrounding shops, restaurants and jogging park were beautifully decorated with colorful, bright lights. It was hard to believe a new year was just a week away.

When Nolan had arrived home from his cousin Lee's wedding, he hadn't bothered to remove his tuxedo. Instead he'd headed straight for the refrigerator, grabbed a beer and proceeded to the balcony for a bit of mental relaxation. But all his mind could do was recall the moment his ninetysomething-year-old great-grandmother, Felicia Laverne Madaris, had finally cornered him at the reception that evening. She was a notorious matchmaker, and he'd been avoiding her all night. Her success rate was too astounding to suit him—and she had calmly warned him that he was next.

He was just as determined not to be.

Nolan, his brother, Corbin, and his cousins Reese and Lee had all been born within a fifteen-month period. They were as close as brothers and had been thick as thieves while growing up. Mama Laverne swore her goal was to marry them all off before she took her last breath. They all told her that wouldn't happen, but then the next thing they knew, Reese had married Kenna and today Lee married Carly.

What bothered Nolan more than anything about his great-grandmother setting her schemes on him was that she of all people knew what he'd gone through with Andrea Dunmire. Specifically, the hurt, pain and humiliation she had caused him. Yes, it had been years ago and he had gotten over it, but there were some things you didn't forget. A woman ripping your heart out of your chest was one of them.

His cell phone rang. Recognizing the ringtone, he pulled it out of his pocket and answered, "Yes, Corbin?"

"Hey, man, I just wanted to check on you. We saw you tear out of here like the devil himself was after you. It's Christmas and we thought you would stay the night at Whispering Pines and continue to party like the rest of us."

Whispering Pines was their uncle Jake's ranch. Nolan took another sip of his beer before saying, "I couldn't stay knowing Mama Laverne is already plotting my downfall. You wouldn't believe what she told me."

"We weren't standing far away and heard."

Nolan shook his head in frustration. "So now all of you know that Mama Laverne's friend's granddaughter is the woman she's picked out for me."

"Yes, and we got a name. Reese and I overheard Mama Laverne tell Aunt Marilyn that your future wife's name is Ivy Chapman."

"Like hell the woman is my future wife." And Nolan couldn't care less about her name. He'd never met her and didn't intend to. "All this time I thought Mama Laverne was plotting to marry the woman's granddaughter off to Lee. She set me up real good."

Corbin didn't say anything and Nolan was glad because for the moment he needed the silence. It didn't matter to him one iota that so far every one of his cousins whose wives had been selected by his great-grandmother were madly in love with their spouses and saw her actions as a blessing and not a curse. What mattered was that she should not have interfered in the process. And what bothered him more than anything was knowing that he was next on her list. He didn't want her to find him a wife. When and if he was ready for marriage, he was certainly capable of finding one on his own.

"You've come up with a plan?" Corbin interrupted Nolan's thoughts to ask.

Nolan thought of the diabolical plan his cousin Lee had put in place to counteract their great-grandmother's shenanigans and guaranteed to outsmart Mama Laverne for sure. However, in the end, Lee's plan had backfired.

"No, why waste my time planning anything? I simply refuse to play the games Mama Laverne is intent on playing. What I'm going to do is ignore her foolishness and enjoy my life as the newest eligible Madaris bachelor."

He could say that since, at thirty-four, he was ten months older than Corbin, who would be next on their great-grandmother's hit list. "By the time I make my rounds, there won't be a single woman living in Houston who won't know I'm not marriage material," Nolan added.

Corbin chuckled. "That sounds like a plan to me."

"Not a plan, just stating my intentions. I refuse to let Mama Laverne shove a wife that I don't want down my throat just because she thinks she can and that she should."

After ending the call with his brother, Nolan swallowed the last of his beer. Like he'd told Corbin, he didn't have a plan and wouldn't waste time coming up with one. What he intended to do was to have fun; as much fun as any single man could possibly have.

A huge smile touched his lips as he left the balcony. Walking into his condo, he headed for his bedroom. Quickly removing the tux, he changed into a pair of slacks and a pullover sweater. The night was still young and there was no reason for him not to go out and celebrate the holiday.

As he moved toward his front door, he started humming "Jingle Bells." *Let the fun begin.*

One

Fifteen months later...

Nolan clicked off his mobile phone, satisfied with the call he'd just ended with Lee about his cousin's newest hotel, the Grand MD Paris. Construction of the huge mega-structure had begun three weeks ago. Already it was being touted by the media as the hotel of the future, and Nolan would have to agree.

Due to the hotel's intricate design and elaborate formation, the estimated completion time was two years. You couldn't rush grandeur, and by the time the doors opened, the Grand MD Paris would set itself apart as one of the most luxurious hotels in the world.

This would be the third hotel Lee and his business partner, DeAngelo Di Meglio, had built. First there had been

the Grand MD Dubai, and after such astounding success
with that hotel, the pair had opened the Grand MD Vegas.
Since both hotels had been doing extremely well finan-
cially, a decision was made to build a third hotel in Paris.
The Grand MD Paris would use state-of-the-art technology while maintaining the rich architectural designs Paris
was known for.

Slade, the architect in the Madaris family, had designed all three Grand MD hotels. Nolan would have
to say that Slade's design of the Paris hotel was nothing short of a masterpiece. Slade had made sure that no
Grand MD hotel looked the same and that each had its
own unique architecture and appeal. Slade's twin, Blade,
was the structural engineer and had spent the last six
months in Paris making sure the groundwork was laid
before work on the hotel began. There had been surveys
that needed to be completed, soil samples to analyze, as
well as a tight construction schedule if they were to meet
the deadline for a grand opening two years from now.
And knowing Lee and DeAngelo like he did, Nolan expected the Grand MD Paris to open its doors on time and
to a fanfare of the likes of a presidential inauguration.

After getting a master's graduate degree at MIT,
Nolan had begun working for Chenault Electronics at
their Chicago office. Chenault Electronics was considered one of the top ten electronics companies in the
world. The owner, Nicholas Chenault, was a family
friend, had taken Nolan under his wing and had not
only been his boss but his mentor, as well.

After working for Chenault for eight years, Nolan

had returned to Houston three years ago to start his
own company, Madaris Innovations.

Nolan's company would provide all the electronic and
technology work for the Grand MD Paris; some would
be the first of its kind anywhere. All high-tech and trend
changing. It would be Nolan's first project of this caliber
and he appreciated Lee and DeAngelo for giving him the
opportunity. Lee and his wife, Carly, spent most of their
time in Paris now. Since DeAngelo and his wife, Peyton,
were expecting their first child four months from now,
DeAngelo had decreased his travel schedule somewhat.

Nolan also appreciated Nicholas for agreeing to partner
with him on the project. Chenault Electronics would be
bringing years of experience and know-how to the table
and Nolan welcomed Nicholas's skill and knowledge.

Nolan had enjoyed the two weeks he'd spent in Paris.
He would have to go back a number of times this year for
more meetings and he looked forward to doing so, since
Paris was one of his favorite places to visit. There was
a real possibility that he might have to live there while
his electronic equipment was scheduled to be installed.

Nolan leaned back in his chair. In a way, he regretted
returning to Houston. Before leaving, he had done everything in his power to become the life of every party, and
his reputation as Houston's number one playboy had been
cemented. In some circles, he'd been pegged as Houston's
One-Night Stander. Now that he was back, that role had to
be rekindled, but if he was honest with himself, he wasn't
looking forward to the nights of mindless, emotionless
sex with women whose names he barely remembered.
He only hoped that Ivy Chapman, her grandmother and

his great-grandmother were getting the message—he had no intentions of settling down anytime soon. At least not in the next twenty-five years or so.

He rubbed a hand down his face, thinking that while he wouldn't admit to it, he was discovering that living the life of a playboy wasn't all that it was cracked up to be. Most of his dates were one-night stands. There were times he would spend a week with the same woman, and occasionally someone would make it a month, but he didn't want to give these women the wrong idea about the possibility of a future together. He was probably going to have to change his phone number due to the number of messages from women wanting a callback. Women expecting a callback. Women he barely remembered from one sexual encounter to the next. Jeez.

Nolan wondered how his cousins Clayton and Blade, the ones who'd been known as die-hard womanizers in the family before they'd settled down to marry, had managed it all. Clayton had had such an active sex life that he'd owned a case of condoms that he'd kept in his closet. Nolan knew that tidbit was more fact than fiction, since he'd seen the case after Clayton had passed it on to Blade when Clayton had gotten married.

Blade hadn't passed the box on to anyone when he'd married. Not only had he used up the case he'd gotten from Clayton, but he'd gone through a case of his own. Somehow Clayton and Blade had not only managed to handle the playboy life, but each claimed they'd enjoyed doing so immensely at the time.

Nolan, on the other hand, was finding the life of a

Casanova pretty damn taxing and way too demanding. And it wasn't even deterring Ivy Chapman.

Nolan picked up the envelope on top of the stack on his desk. He knew what it was and who it had come from. He recalled getting the first one six months ago and he had received several more since then. He wondered why Ivy Chapman was still sending him these little personal notes when he refused to acknowledge them. All the notes said the same thing... *Nolan, I would love to meet you. Call me so it can be arranged. Here is my number...*

Nolan didn't give a royal flip what her phone number was, since he had no intentions of calling her, regardless of the fact that his matchmaking great-grandmother fully expected him to do so. He would continue to ignore Miss Chapman and any correspondence she sent him. He refused to give in to his great-grandmother's matchmaking shenanigans.

He tossed the envelope aside and picked up his cell phone to call his family and let them know he was back. He had slept off jet lag most of yesterday and hadn't talked to anyone other than his cousin Reese and his brother, Corbin. Reese and his wife, Kenna, were expecting their first baby in June and everyone was excited. For years, Reese and Kenna, who'd met in college, had claimed they were nothing but best friends. However, the family had known better and figured one day the couple would reach the same conclusion. Mama Laverne bragged that they were just another one of her success stories.

Nolan ended the call with his parents, stood and walked over to the window to look out. Like most of his relatives, he leased space in the Madaris Building. His

He was going to win the game. Once and for all. And the woman he hoped would be his trump card was on her way.

The doorbell rang and he stood up behind his desk. She was here. And she was—he checked his watch—late.

A half smile curved his lips.

Perfect.

He took the stairs two at a time. He was impatient to meet his temporary bride. Impatient to get this plan started so it could end.

He strode across the entryway and jerked the door open. And froze.

The woman standing on his porch was small. And young, just as he'd expected, but… She wore no makeup, which made her look like a damned teenager. Her features were fine and pointed; her dark brown hair hung lank beneath a ragged beanie that looked like it was in the process of unraveling while it sat on her head.

He didn't bother to linger over the rest of the details—her threadbare sweater with too-long sleeves, her tragic skinny jeans—because he was stopped, immobilized really, by the tiny bundle in her arms.

A baby.

His prospective bride had come with a baby.

Well, hell.

Want to give in to temptation with
steamy tales of irresistible desire?

Check out **Harlequin® Presents®,
Harlequin® Desire** and
Harlequin® Kimani™ Romance books!

New books available every month!

CONNECT WITH US AT:

Harlequin.com/Community

 Facebook.com/HarlequinBooks

 Twitter.com/HarlequinBooks

 Instagram.com/HarlequinBooks

 Pinterest.com/HarlequinBooks

ReaderService.com

**ROMANCE WHEN
YOU NEED IT**

PGENRE2017